Fleeting Moments

Fleeting Moments

an anthology

Talisman

This collection copyright © Talisman 2012.
Copyright in the text reproduced herein remains the
property of the individual authors, and permission
to publish is gratefully acknowledged by the editors
and publishers.

British Library Cataloguing in Publication Data

A Record of this Publication is available from the British
Library

ISBN 978-0-9568680-5-3

This edition published 2012 by Talisman
Manchester, England

Phoenix Writers gratefully acknowledges the financial
assistance of Bolton CVS, Bolton Arts Forum, Horwich
Town Council and Mrs Helen Smith towards the
production of this anthology.

Cover design and images: Pam Hunter
Logo design : David Lawson
Editing: Robert and Claire Yates

All Talisman books are published on paper derived from
sustainable resources.

For Robert Smith
who inspired us
'to feel the music of the present.'

Contents

Foreword – Today's the Day

Desk facing the wall – no distractions. Notes – check, printer working – check. Here goes.

Ding – dong

Ignore – you're not expecting anyone. But suppose it's... Might be a parcel, then it's more time wasted having to collect it. Quickly, run.

Crate of wine for next door. Good idea that, having it delivered, saves time. Might just Google the company...

NO – STOP – GET ON WITH IT!

Right. Title, double spacing, font. Which font? Times New Roman – boring. Ariel – can look okay. How about Courier? Makes it look like a proper manuscript.

STOP MESSING AROUND – GET TYPING!

Phone on silent. Hang on, there's a text. *Need PE kit – trying out for team. LOL. Darling Daughter.* Should have thought of that before school – tough. But the team...

Can't let them all down, can she? Keys...

Had no idea the tank was on empty – could have done without that queue at Tesco's. Always seem to be behind someone who decides to do their weekly shop in the One Stop whilst they're paying. I need a brew...

Washing out – can't waste a good drying day, can I? Now where was I...?

Barney, is that you? Good boy, do you want to go in the garden? That's a horrible noise, sounds like you're going to be... No, please, no. Great. Right, where's the shovel and some newspaper? What a stink. I give up...

Most writers will identify with this scenario when, just as you are about to sit down and begin your literary masterpiece, events conspire to put everything in your way to prevent you. When eventually you get that precious moment, you then experience the fickle nature of the creative muse; those wonderful ideas that were clamouring like small children around your ankles have disappeared into the ether like wraiths.

However, our writers have managed to find the time to take home the carefully planted seedlings of ideas created during our weekly sessions, nurtured them, and let them grow into pieces of writing that we want now to share with you.

So this is your opportunity to take a little 'down time', put your feet up, relax and browse our anthology.

Enjoy.

Claire Yates

Do Not Be Afraid

Insignificance, allowing greater forces to inspire,
Gives existence to the universal being,
The unimagined energies, which fill the quasars
And are picked up here from the edge of time.
Matter is sucked into black holes into who
Knows where.
The atoms that make us will go on a journey,
They are part of common reality,
Though life's imprint is so tiny and so brief
The moment will always be there.
There is no such thing as nothing—
Even the emptiest space is active,
Be it pulsating quantum froth
Or the full-on blast of x-rays
From as far as we can see.

Because of this do not be afraid of the future,
Feel the music of the present.

Robert Smith

Mrs Day

The old lady worries. She tells her friends she's spent her whole life worrying ; but that *isn't* true because she is 92, and still has most of her faculties intact, including her hearing, mind, and wits. Walking is more difficult, however, and she has to give herself more time to get everywhere, and her eyesight isn't quite what it was.

But she's worrying a little at the moment – just a smidgen, and the last thing she wants now is palpitations, like an over-wound watch.

She's had time to reflect whilst being alone. She knows her body-clock must be nearly at midnight, especially as her own mother died at 60, and her dad had been a year younger. But they had died in an accident so sometimes she has rationalised that their body-clocks were only just past 12 midday. Hour-glasses smashed half-full, *not* half-empty.

She peers at her watch... well, her mother's watch really, so it must be very old, but it still keeps perfect time, and the habit of winding it each day keeps her fingers nimble, and she delights that she can still hear its reassuring tick. Now, might be as good a time as any to telephone.

Her fingers manage the keypad easily. 'Hello,' she says. 'I'm ringing about Mrs. Day. She's—'

'Just a moment.'

The old lady waits. How long is a moment? She idly wonders whether all moments are the same length.

'Hello, Staff Nurse Williams here. Can I help you?'

A flicker of a smile creases the old lady's face and the wrinkles ripple. Progress. 'I hope so. I'm enquiring about

Mrs. Day… **MRS. DAY.** You know her. She was admitted three days ago, was it?'

'Just a moment…'

The smile fades, like someone has drawn the blinds. She tries to listen. She's told her great-great grandchildren that she can hear a pin drop *on the carpet!* She loves their laugh in response, and has said to herself that she'd like to record it and have the tape in her coffin one day. But not yet!

Snatches of conversation reach her. 'Mrs Day… the old dear…' 'Her in the side ward, B1, is it?'… 'Anyone seen her notes?' The old lady waits. Despite being the teeniest bit worried at this precise moment, she's actually patient. *'Patience is a virtue'* is something she's lived by for 92 years. It's done her no harm.

Staff Nurse Williams' voice returns: 'Hello. Found them… Um… Mrs. Day's a lot better. Her infection has cleared. Temperature down. Pulse back to normal. Everything OK. Back to normal, I should think. Good for her age, actually. Can go home today. Receptionist just needs to organise everything… Can I tell her you called?'

The old lady smiles again. 'Not really.' She pauses, wondering what the nurse might be thinking. 'You see, I actually *am* the old dear in B1! Good for her age, actually! It's just that nobody bothers to pop in to tell you anything in this place! But thank you!'

Martin Rimmington

Heat of the Moment

(Inspired by the painting **Moroccan Garden** by Frederick J. Porter, Bolton Art Gallery)

The gun presses against Clive's thigh; he grazes its outline with one hand, checks his Patek Phillipe. Three thirty. Not long now. Faint sounds trickle in from the outside world, breaching the thick stone walls surrounding the garden. A man's voice strung tight with doubt, challenged by a female tirade that grows louder and louder until halted by the definitive slam of a door. Clive gives a wry smile.

'Poor sod.'

He is standing in the darker of two archways that lie along the underbelly of the ancient house. Further along, two wooden benches with thin faded cushions offer weary visitors respite from the heat. His fingertips trace hairline cracks running zigzags across the terracotta bricks; the mortar crumbles at his touch, leaving fine powdery trails along the creases of his palm. Across the courtyard a fountain bubbles and fizzes in the sunshine, its glistening droplets cascading into a shallow marble bowl. A solitary lizard rests on its lip, still as death. As Clive watches, one reptilian eyeball flickers, betraying life. In the same moment the lizard shimmers, vanishes into an invisible fissure, slick as oil. Beyond the fountain Clive sees a leggy palm. Head and shoulders above the rest, it strains over the far wall, nodding at unseen events.

Beads of sweat pop along Clive's spine, dampening his linen shirt. Where is she, damn it? Three forty, still no show. He arrived in good time, anticipating her arrival. Everything is set; he wants this over and done with. The

15

urge for a cool Peroni rasps at his parched throat, and he aches for the comfort of a cigarette, that calming heady rush of nicotine.

The lizard skitters out into the sunshine, skin flashing turquoise, alert. Somewhere a latch clicks and a shadow advances along the shaft of exposed light, metal heels ring out across the tiles. He flattens himself against the pillar, hearing desiccated leaves crackle as tiny creatures scuttle to safety.

Clive wipes his hand on a white laundered handkerchief, rests it tenderly on the pistol butt, thumb ready on the safety catch.

'Who's there?' she demands, sliding Gucci sunglasses slowly down the elegant slope of her nose as she scans the courtyard. Satisfied, she slides the black leather holdall off her shoulder, rests it on the fountain's edge. Slowly, she unzips it.

Raising the gun to shoulder height Clive steps, blinking, into the sunlight. He stands for a moment admiring her tanned arms, her waist cinched in a figure-hugging dress. Her polished lenses reflect a convex view of the garden and give nothing away.

'What are you hoping to do with that?' Her words are laced with Latino, rich and dark as the Torres brandy she favours. A smile flits across scarlet lips.

'What do you suggest?' Clive moves towards her, contracting the space between them. The air near the fountain feels cool and fresh, despite the heat. He places the gun between two delicate ribs, slides her glasses up to rest on ebony hair. Her eyes flash emerald.

'Careful with that thing darling, you might hurt someone.' She reaches down to push the barrel away with one scarlet-tipped finger.

Clive slips the safety catch on, laughs. He cups her elbow and together they lean over the bag, parted to reveal the two paintings, expertly separated from their frames with a scalpel, now secreted in the front pocket of the holdall alongside her fake ID badge and two passports.

Three fifty five.

Plenty of time to reach their client's private airstrip, just outside the city. With the alarm system down, no-one will discover the loss until the gallery re-opens at five. Clive takes her hand in his as they leave the courtyard; behind them the lizard, motionless, absorbs the afternoon's heat.

Claire Yates

Yesterday I Bought a Ticket

I bought a ticket yesterday, on a bus
For a while, I owned a ticket
That ticket was mine
I had a seat, I had a seat on that bus
I was on.
Where are they now? That bus, that seat, that ticket.
I had a small child, once. A house, then another
Houses, gardens, fences. Pens and poems
They have gone from me now,
I own them no more.

The ink in the pen runs out
The light in the day fades into night. Look!
The oval mirror, 'that's mine!' I've had it for years,
Yet I look into it and that face that looked
Years ago, has changed, gone
I do not own that face,
This face.
Complete is my un-ownership.

I bought a ticket yesterday.

Vicky Adshead

Fairy Ring

This morning: blackbird notes, a fairy ring.
Could I, should I
Take magic eyes,
Miniaturise, eat male fern seed,
Tiptoe past guardians of invisibility?
Find hiding under tufts of grass:
Upturned flowerpots, blackbird's wing,
Fairies meet with elven feet.

But sun's blade pierces
This eerie state—
And I am otherworld dazzled.

Pam Hunter

I walk on white bones.
Bleached by tireless sun they break,
Crumbling to dust.
I polish, pocket a tooth
And lift my face to the light.

Claire Yates

A Fine Romance

MONDAY: 7 a.m.

Grace draws her coat to in an attempt to keep out the cool breeze. She climbs the steps to the platform and joins the other commuters. Twisting her scarf once more round her neck she surveys the crowd as if searching for someone. The train arrives, everyone surges forward. They pause briefly to allow the cheerful woman in the black anorak and trousers to alight. This is a daily occurrence; it is an automatic movement, an arrival and departure in reverse. There he is, the man in the pin-striped suit and black shiny shoes. He is hurling himself towards them. To her satisfaction he has a look of George Clooney. The door closes as he seats himself opposite her and gazes out of the window at the passing brewery.

MONDAY: 7 a.m.

Alan curses as he hurries up the steps and throws himself through the open door. He makes a memo to himself to arrive earlier in future if only to pick up a copy of the Metro. She is already in the corner with her bag positioned on the adjoining seat as if to ward off strangers. Her sideways glance, not quite in his direction, with a hint of a smile, he finds most attractive. The way in which her right hand goes to her throat to adjust her scarf tells him that she is not over confident. He wonders about the exact colour of her eyes. Certainly that pink jumper with the purplish scarf suits her. He looks out of the window so as to allay suspicion.

TUESDAY: 7 a.m.

Grace swivels her head and nods to her fellow passengers on reaching the platform. He's leaving it until the last minute again. Perhaps his wife is to blame. She decides to examine the third finger of his left hand when the opportunity arises. Maybe it's his meticulous attention to his shoes that delays him. Good, he's heading for her compartment. That way she'll be able to study him more closely. Same suit, different shirt. That light blue is a better choice than the dark checked affair of the previous day. Shame about the tie though. Probably a Christmas present from an elderly aunt.

TUESDAY: 7 a.m.

Alan promises himself that in future he'll clean his shoes the night before. It's that last minute shine that somehow delays him. If the train arrived early he'd miss it. He flings himself into the compartment ensuring that he has an uninterrupted view of her. Yes, she's tall but not too tall. She would fit comfortably under his arm he is sure, although a seated person can give a distorted impression of his or her height. He thinks that her eyes are green, well, greenish. There's something different about her hair today. She's swept it to one side. He likes it that way.

WEDNESDAY: 7 a.m.

Grace hooks her bag onto her shoulder before becoming aware that he is already at the top of the steps. This is an improvement. The train is not due for another five minutes. He gives a nod in her direction. He's really quite good looking in a subtle sort of way. Standing a short distance away, he is shuffling from one foot to another. Surely he's not nervous near her. As he stands aside to let her board before him, she gives him an extra point for good manners. It's a more acceptable tie today as well. There's no ring or even a tell-tale white mark in its place. She wonders what he does for a living. On arrival at the final station she fumbles in her bag as if searching for her ticket. In this way she is able to scrutinise his back as he disappears into the crowd ahead of her. Yes, he is certainly a good few inches taller than her.

WEDNESDAY: 7 a.m.

Alan sighs. He's made it with time to spare. It was worth the last minute rush. She has acknowledged his nod and is smiling back at him. Without doubt she's pretty and today she's wearing a skirt. Just as he suspected, she's got a decent pair of legs. Also wearing a higher pair of heels than usual. He is surprised how much he's noticed about her since Monday. Is that really only two days ago? He gathers his Metro and briefcase together ready to alight. But wait, why is she suddenly rummaging in her bag? Her ticket is in her jacket pocket, he knows. This is becoming embarrassing. He only just manages to stop himself from telling her, but feels that he no longer has any excuse to delay his departure from the carriage.

THURSDAY: 7 a.m.

Grace wonders if she is mistaken. She is almost sure that he was about to speak to her yesterday. All that kerfuffle over her ticket had made her confused and go red.

Wonder of wonders, he's early again today. That's two consecutive days. He smiles at her and mouths a greeting. Is this a sign? The corners of his mouth turn seductively downwards. Wait: is that a dimple in his chin? It's immensely kissable. What a good job it is that he can't read her thoughts. He's picking up a Metro. What on earth does he need that for? Unless it's a cover, a way of looking at her without it being obvious. They enter the train together and sit diagonally opposite each other. The ticket collector approaches. She produces her ticket immediately and holds it out, turning her face away in embarrassment.

THURSDAY: 7 a.m.

Alan looks at his watch. He's early again. When he thinks back to the day before he realises that he missed an opportunity to approach her, talk to her and not just about the whereabouts of her ticket. Any available chance from now on must be taken advantage of. He makes a start by smiling in her direction with a 'Good morning' following on his lips. He picks up a copy of the free newspaper to give himself something to occupy not only his hands, but his mind, while he contemplates his next move. They enter the carriage together but sit separately. On seeing the ticket collector making his way down the compartment, he sneaks a glance at her to see if she recalls what happened yesterday. If he's not mistaken she's blushing.

FRIDAY: 7 a.m.

Grace is pleased that the weather has improved. Today she has put on her new sparkly top and gladiator sandals and has sprayed herself liberally with Dior J'Adore. He is already standing on the platform muttering to himself as if reciting the lines from a script. His eyes catch hers; his gaze lingers longer than is comfortable, Finally she looks away slightly embarrassed. They almost bump into each other as they attempt to get on the train at the same time. He steps back full of apologies. She feels herself attracted, drawn to this fellow passenger. She wishes that he would make a move. She is sure that the attraction is mutual. In her imagination she can picture him coming home to her that very evening, being kissed at the door, presented with a bunch of flowers and a romantic dinner to follow and…

FRIDAY: 7 a.m.

Alan can feel more warmth in the air than earlier in the week. Before long he will be able to change into his light-weight linen suit. Here she comes, there's a different air about her today. She's wearing a top that glitters as she moves and a pair of those Roman type sandals. He can see the pink of her toe nails peeping through the straps. They enter the carriage at almost the same time before he gestures for her to go first, murmuring a 'sorry'. He really does fancy her. This game, idea, call it what you will, has definitely worked. She'd been right and he'd tell her so tonight over the candlelit dinner. 'We need to put the romance back in our marriage,' she'd said, 'go back to flirting with each other.' Yes, he thought, and I must remember to buy a bunch of roses, it was the very least that Grace deserved.

Barbara Oldham

A History Of Time

Justin cursed silently as he discovered yet another small hole in the fabric of Time. It was those blasted moths again, getting into the company's stock rooms and hatching their greedy families in the rolls of exquisitely woven fabrics. He'd been waging war on the pests for weeks now, ever since Eric in Stock Control had first brought the matter to his attention, but nothing either of them did seemed to reduce their numbers, or curb their destructive appetites.

He shook his head in dismay. What would his father say this time? Justin pictured the tired, careworn face of the Managing Director, Mark Time, which was looking more and more hopeless as the weeks passed. This latest assault might be the last straw.

Justin had to admit he too was beginning to feel desperate, yet it wasn't that long ago that he had come of age and had been excited and proud to become a junior partner in the family firm, Time's – now Messrs Time, Father and Son. Then, he had been optimistic and enthusiastic; now, he wasn't sure whether the firm would survive until his next birthday. Holes in their latest collection of fabrics, a particularly expensive batch of their finest cloth, woven with gossamer and silver threads that shimmered in shades of grey, could cost them their national reputation and close the business for good.

Justin sighed as he carefully unrolled and examined the cloth more closely. As the silky material cascaded onto the inspection table, he felt as though history was slipping through his fingers. Time's was a long-established company that had been producing cloth and fine clothing since Immemorial Time, Justin's grandfather, became the first textile merchant to experiment extensively with pure spider silk and the only man ever to weave it to perfection.

Prior to that, production at Time's Textiles had been a rather patchy affair, due to Immemorial's father, Francis T. Time, the founder of the company, being obsessed with using only natural materials. There followed a series of unfortunate failures, notably an attempt to metamorphose the golden sands from the local beach into a knitting yarn. Locals still laughingly referred to the beach as the Sands of Time. No-one could accuse Francis T of not being a trier however, and eventually he hit upon the novel idea of producing a soft, light-weight material woven entirely from local fog.

Justin smiled as he recalled the stories his grandmother had told him about Francis T's commercial venture into fog, which was gathered in season twice yearly on the moors above the mill. It was a risky business to all concerned, but particularly dangerous for the piece workers, as the moors contained fathomless peat bogs that could suck a man down before you could say 'warp and weft.' From being a small boy Justin had heard countless horror tales of fog-gathering and the hardships it had caused in the early years.

And it wasn't simply the gathering of the raw material that had caused problems. The trouble with fog, apart from the obvious difficulty of initial preparation and stabilisation for the looms, is its inconsistency of density, even within the same harvest. Time's had fought hard to overcome these technical challenges, and believed they had succeeded. The garments they produced were sensational and extremely sought-after, establishing Time's Textiles as the foremost weavers and tailors in the business, with a wealthy and illustrious clientele, which included famous celebrities, successful entrepreneurs and members of the aristocracy, both at home and abroad.

However, one year, following what was thought to be a particularly bountiful harvest the previous autumn, a substantial amount of finished cloth unaccountably wore thin very quickly, and led to a large number of disappointed and angry clients, who demanded compensation for wasted Time products.

Even worse, some of the material seemed to dissolve on contact with air after only a few days and simply vanished. City gents suddenly missed the brand new and expensively tailored suit in their wardrobes; in the dressing rooms of rich and fashionable ladies, the latest haute-couture creation was missed from its hanger, much to their distress. (Although it has to be said that in some dressing rooms, where there were more clothes than enough, the garments were not missed for several days). It caused an outrage for miles around and was compounded when news broke that a distant but very high-ranking client had become the latest casualty to what had become known locally as the 'Misseds' of Time, when the dignitary's new suit inexplicably disappeared in the middle of a very public event.

Justin recalled the shock and indignation on his grandmother's face as she told him the story and her outrage when he couldn't stop laughing. 'It was no joke,' she scolded. 'Your great-grandfather's business nearly collapsed there and then.' Justin had apologised and begged her to carry on. And so he learned more of the history of Francis T. Time Textiles.

Ever one to make a profit out of a calamity, Francis' brother Elva, an undertaker, leapt at the opportunity of purchasing the flawed and otherwise useless cloth at a rock bottom price for his own business enterprise; he lined his coffins with the stuff and carefully wrapped his clients in the silvery grey fabric for burial. Thus they became shrouded in the 'Misseds' of Time, but only for a couple of days, as the shrouds soon evaporated leaving Elva's clients rather embarrassingly exposed. Elva realised he would have to work quickly or his business would go under, so to speak, so he forged ahead with an energetic new concept in burials, where speed and efficiency were paramount. His slogan, 'Have an Elva Time when you go!' was painted over the chapel of rest in large gold lettering and was a roaring success. Almost overnight, his funeral parlour became *de rigueur (mortis)* for the deceased and led to a business unparalleled in the county. Elva soon began to enjoy the profits of an increasingly rapid turnover and even lost considerable weight as the slow measured steps of the funeral corteges were hastened to a brisk march.

Justin smiled wryly when he thought about Elva's bodies shrouded in the 'Misseds' of Time and grinned at the irony.

Whilst Elva was busy making his fortune however, Francis T. was rapidly losing his. Once the story of the vanishing garments became public, a queue of furious people demanding compensation formed at his door. Under the onslaught of complaints, threatened lawsuits and looming bankruptcy, Francis T. was desperately trying to find a way out of his predicament. He was even beginning to contemplate suicide, when his younger son, Nick, who was employed in sweeping the weaving sheds clean, had a bright idea; the sheds were plagued by giant spiders and were full of cobwebs – why not use their thread to make a brand new type of cloth? Nick was painfully aware – as his blistered hands and aching muscles bore testament – that the silk produced by these creatures was extremely tough and strong; Nick knew from bitter experience the very last thing it would do was spontaneously disappear.

It has to be said that Nick's idea didn't exactly stem from a noble desire to rescue the business, nor even to save his father from killing himself; killing Time senior was an idea Nick had been toying with himself, ever since his father had put him to work at the age of thirteen in what Nick considered even then to be a very junior and demeaning role. Now aged twenty-two, Nick realised he had the indelible marks of Time on his hands as years of blisters had hardened and become ugly, rough calluses. No wonder he had never managed to go out with any of the local girls for more than a week; they never got beyond holding hands. Nick's future was looking decidedly singular, but this creative flash of inspiration could resolve his blisters, his love life and might even lead to a more dignified position in the family firm.

He spoke to Immemorial.

Immemorial was impressed. Until now, his opinion of his younger brother was based purely on the amount of complaining he did each evening and his inordinate use of scented hand cream. Could Nick have come up with something totally brilliant? He beamed at his brother and hugged him enthusiastically, promising him a better deal in the future and recognition of his great idea – if it worked – with his name emblazoned on the waving sheds – 'Nick of Time's Textiles – Weaving Division.'

Immemorial knew he would now have to persuade his stubborn, blinkered old-fashioned father to move with one of the junior Times; it would be a difficult task. Francis T carefully controlled his sons' involvement in the business, giving them virtually no corporate responsibility. But now with the company heading for disaster, Immemorial was desperate for a seat on the Board; he would demand to be part of Time Management.

With the hounds of the press baying ever louder for blood over the scandal of the disappearing clothing, Immemorial forced his father to face some of the outrageous headlines – 'Time for an unexpected change?' 'Police Chief in Indecent Exposure,' 'Time – Naked Truth Revealed' and 'A Bum Deal?' – to name but a few. When shock tactics didn't work, Immemorial resorted to simple emotional blackmail. He pointed out that Francis T's inaction or his suicide would amount to the same thing – the whole family would be plunged into poverty and with no-one knowing how to run the business, Time's as they knew it would end.

And in any case, Immemorial would entrust his father's funeral arrangements to Elva.

Horrified, Francis T. made him Managing Director with immediate effect, and quietly retired to Switzerland, where he continued to indulge his passion for combining natural resources with modern technology by inventing a clock which used live birds to announce the hours.

By the end of a fortnight, Immemorial and Nick had the first batch of silk cloth ready for the tailors.

Silk cloth, silk cloth... Justin's wandering mind suddenly swung back to the present and the material in his hands. Silk cloth. Immemorial's stroke of genius that saved the company from disaster years before was now itself the very object of attack! The firm's future was once again at stake.

Justin examined the holes in the material once more.

The more he looked, the more astonished he became. The holes were quite neatly and regularly made, and scattered fairly uniformly across the entire width of the cloth. In fact, as Justin shook the roll out, he could have sworn they formed a pattern of sorts, and not an unpleasing one at that. With a bit of inventiveness and some cunning advertising slogans, they might just get away with it. In fact, the more he thought about it, the more excited he became as he realised they'd hit upon a totally new product!

He called the Chief Designer, Imogen Nation, to come and look at the cloth.

Imogen was as enthusiastic as Justin. 'But it's absolutely fantastic!' she cried, examining the neat holes. 'We could embroider around the holes in silver thread to make the most luxurious material for ladies' evening wear, or use silk multi-coloured threads running across the lace pattern to give a bright, modern textured effect. There are all sorts of possibilities. What do you think, Justin?'

'I think you're brilliant,' beamed Justin. 'A stitch in Time's best cloth is going to be the most successful idea for this company yet!' Then for a moment, Justin's face grew serious. 'You know, when I first saw the holes, I really thought it was the worst of Time's; now it will be the best of Time's, and it's all thanks to you, Imogen, my Chief Designer and Superstar!' Imogen grinned as Justin grabbed her and swung her round the room in a triumphant dance. He whooped for joy, a ridiculous smile on his face. 'Time's goes on!' he cried. 'Time's waits for no man! Yeeha!'

And to this day Time's warp and weft are still creating their rich and colourful tapestries.

Anne Lawson

Whence Comes This Fancy?

Whence comes this fancy,
These notes,
This art,

From where, for whom?
Out of the disturbing firmament,
The chemistry of minds,

Or some random,
Hopelessly unknown
Firing of neurones.

Some do say
That only when the soul is well
Will they have the least effect.

When he walks in black,
Bent before the indifferent world,
No ray shall touch him,

No lengthening of day
Shall catch his mood.
Only the full-throated storm,

Loud, defiant,
At odds with all,
Would lead him on.

Robert Smith

Playtime

Nail-bitten kids,
Shoes toe-scuffed bare,
Race, hop, charge
Within the metal-spiked
Ringed yard of tarmac.

Joyous shrieks escape, rise
Like balloons, drift into the distance
Away from bedlam's anarchy
Of energy, till the bell
Or whistle summonses the panting
Learners to line up quickly, in rows –
'No jostling please!'
Ready again, just, for class rules.

Martin Rimmington

Standing Still

Early morning mist unfurls across blunt stubble. A lone rabbit stops in its tracks by the lightning tree, white scut trembling in anticipation. The moment passes and it lollops along the earth boundary, pausing to nibble at tender blades of grass. Further down the field a rainbow of diesel trails towards a metal gate looped shut with orange twine. Beyond this, from the silhouette of the woods, a vixen calculates distance, speed, size of prey.

The sun begins to haul itself over the sloe stained hills, stretching thin fingers across the furrows where plumes of steam rise from the damp loam, and further, to meet gnarled roots that sprawl out from the base of the thicket. In the farmyard on the far side of the trees a cock crows, shrill, and the hens mutter their muted response.

The rabbit has gone now, hotfoot, tunneled deep inside its burrow. The fox's stomach contracts and she turns to her cubs hidden in twisted undergrowth, her nose twitching as she picks up the faint scent of a field mouse.

The farmer yawns as he strolls across the yard. Stops, stretches, rubs his belly, hauls himself into the cab. The tractor fires first time; a smile spreads across his weathered face, revealing teeth like oak stumps. He pulls his cap down, shielding his eyes against the rising sun before chugging slowly up the track, avoiding ancient ruts.

Claire Yates

The Face in the Wall

The face in the wall watched all that went on and did not approve. The disapproval was expressed subtly at first, a mere flicker of admonition through a slight smudging of outlines as the face hardened about the forehead spreading downwards to that mouth.

Then as they carried on without care, without conscience, the face released the hardness and let one colour run into another, darkening the red, deepening the black, spreading a stain that George noticed because he was so alone these days. All days in fact, now that his Aunt was gone. Indeed if George hadn't had the face to look at now, he doubted very much if anyone would have noticed him at all. Looking at someone else was a skill, it really was. It took time and care, and all these things seemed of the past nowadays, for with his Aunt's death, the world's eyes had fallen away. In this sightless place he wandered through her house each day, listening to the faint, hoarse whispering of dark suited men with snapping brief cases, and the click clack of women with narrow eyes devouring papers which promised so much they believed, yet so far had delivered so very, very little.

George's father stood at the front door of his late sister's house, carelessly smoking as he had always done, watching them all, smiling at their hopes which grew like grey tentacles about the house, choking at the heart of George's Aunt who now stood in turn powerless, watching them back, praying the face in the wall could heal that which her soul could not.

George smelt the scent of greed along the corridors of his Aunt's old home. Each carpet held a pattern that seemed to tell him more about these figures that lay littering the tables in the kitchen pored over by eyes which would never return a look. Greed had a humming sound, a chorus insinuated itself upwards to the attics, to this gallery where George would sit reading, where he felt comfortable enough to remember his Aunt, a memory he knew, beyond doubt, this face in the wall knew as well as he.

George's favourite memory was of soap. She had loved yellow tar soap and they had washed her last dog together under the yard tap whilst she told him about Carmen and the colours around his head, and why he must never ever forget Demeter. Cluedo had shook herself all over him, splashing the tar all over his bare arms and then just when they had been talking about her, Demeter had arrived back from somewhere and had pulled his hair and he knew he was alive.

George did not know how to talk to Demeter. She walked across the lawn towards him like a miracle. The late afternoon sunshine on her red hair whiplashed his face and he felt the tips of his fingers burn with the energy of her. He was dazed by her mouth; he wanted to cross himself at the power of her, he wanted to lift her hair away from her long neck and kiss her madly so she would never forget his name.

But he was just a boy. A boy who had a soft voice that made kind people lean towards him as he tried to speak of his Aunt. He felt his voice was borrowed today. It was on hire somehow and could be recalled at any moment. And as he spoke it was as if he was waiting for his words to be snatched away; so he released them slowly, each word a sharply shaped pebble for listeners to turn around in their hands. There were corners to each word.

Hello then Demeter.

What an uneven boy she thought. Uneven, and suddenly tender. And there she saw him again holding his aunt's hand, purely and only for her.

Janet Lewison

Vessel

Today, I start coiling a new pot. I take some clay and knead it until it is pliable in the way that I used to watch my mother and grandmother do so many times. The work is familiar for it seems I have made pots all my life. I learned first by watching my mother, Kali, and grandmother, Maga, who was known as Little Gazelle, for the grace of her movements. I too am called Maga. I was born in a village on the shores of Lake Malawi, the enchantress of my childhood who still haunts my dreams. All the women in my village were graceful, balancing heavy pots on their heads with a natural deportment that seemed to defy gravity. I remember the first pot I ever made and the words my grandmother spoke when I gave it to her.

'It is beautiful, little Maga,' she said, 'but even the Yawo women would have trouble balancing this pot on their heads.'

I add some more coils and pull up the clay from inside, creating volume and thinning the clay wall − its skin or membrane − from inside; already I begin to feel the beating of its heart. This thin wall divides the inner and the outer space. Grandmother Maga, the best potter in our village, taught me how to create a pot with this sensitivity, for it is when the tension between inner and outer form is finely balanced that the pot assumes a resonance, a presence, and seems to occupy a greater space than it physically displaces. The vessel is all about containment and displacement. The clay and I begin to communicate, whisper secrets to one another. It reveals its own unique qualities and strength, for it has taken countless millennia to form. I take my own time, for it will not be rushed, this process. Mother showed me how each part of the pot is named after the body and, laughing, I would point to my own body parts as she named them for me: foot, belly, neck, lip. That sense of fun has never left me, for it is a joy to create. This pot is for her.

Mother and I left Malawi many years ago and came to England. It was hard at first but we gradually adjusted. I won a scholarship to study ceramics at Cambridge college of art with the great Ladi Kwali and so my career began and today my pots are also sought after. More importantly I could afford to take mother home to Malawi to see the Little Gazelle one last time. I took her the pot I had made for her and waited. She, too, had remembered.

'It is truly beautiful, Maga,' she told me, 'and though it is true it would give our Yawo women some trouble, it too has a balance that seems to defy gravity.'

Pam Hunter

Geneva Nights

A Sketch Uncut

CAST

Didi – 13, indeterminate gender

Cop

Big Bonus – in long, black coat, collar up and hat

Didi is juggling with two apples and an orange.

Did. – Why do I live in the most uncool town on the planet?

Cop – Geneva? Good place to be a cop: not many villains, and everybody driving like angels. Bloke called Calvin wrote the rules, called it the City of God.

Did. – The no-dog-shit city.

Cop – It's quite interesting underground.

Did. – Gas pipes – I sometimes think about that, when I light my gas rings, think about the flame going down the pipe. Could the gas burn inside the pipes, all the way back to where it comes from, burning all the houses and offices and all the city. And the banks? That would be quite interesting.

Cop – It's so peaceful tonight.

Did. – Dead.

Cop – I did have a traffic accident yesterday. Driver collided with a cyclist.

Did. – Anybody dead?

Cop – Driver said he didn't see him, said he just fell out of the sky. Cyclist said he couldn't remember anything so he might have fallen from the sky. He told me to put that in my report – 'I fell down from the sky.'

Did. – Have an apple.

Cop – Didn't mean gas pipes.

Did. – What?

Cop – When I said it was more interesting underground. There's the Collider.

Did. – The Large Hadron Collider, great big, round tunnel. Why's it called a collider?

Cop – They fire these invisible sub-atomic particles to collide with each other, round and round, nearly the speed of light. (*demonstrates*) When two collide, like these apples, you might discover a totally new kind of particle.

Did. – Like an orange.

Cop – Trying to find a particle called Higgs Boson. Somebody called it the God Particle coz it's supposed to solve the contradictions between Relativity and Quantum physics... I think. Funny that...

Did. – What's funny?

Cop – The geezer on the bike, when I asked him his name, I'm sure he said it was Higgs Boson. He definitely said that: Mr. Higgs Boson.

Did. – Might have said, bike's broken... Or BIG BONUS.

Cop – He was stunned though.

Enter Big Bonus with suitcase bearing legend in big letters 'BIG BONUS'

Did. – He's behind you!

Cop – Good morning sir, let me help you with that.

The suitcase is heavy, Bonus is out of breath but he shrugs away the offer of help and sits with his back to the audience.

Cop – I was saying. They reckon one of these days, when two particles collide it might make a black hole and we'll all be swallowed by gravity, turned into anti-matter, all of Switzerland.

Did. – Cool!

Cop – All that money turned into anti-matter.

Did. – What…?

Cop – When I said it's more interesting underground I didn't mean gas pipes. And I didn't mean the Collider.

Did. – What then?

Cop – All that treasure in those bank vaults down there.

Did. – All that loot stashed away by the Nazis…

Cop – No, that's a trifle compared to what's coming in now. We've got cash underground that's been nicked from everybody in the world…

Did. – In the most law-abiding country in the world?

Cop – All legal, they're all doing it, banks, corporations, and…

Did – *(Indicates Big Bonus)* He's listening

Cop – *(whispering)* Googols of cash.

Did. – Googols?

Cop – Google it – 'Gooooooooooooooooooogols!' All should have been paid in taxes. Something called the Deficit. They're all getting in on it – Boots, McDonald's, Cadbury's, (have a crème egg), Tesco – The Deficit's right under your feet.

Did. – All that loot nestled up to the Collider. Think, if

43

one infinitesimally tiny particle – so small nobody noticed it was there, a trouble-maker, a dysfunctional, sociopathic, anarchist, particle with an ASBO and body odor collided with… with… *(strikes the apples together and we have thunder and lightning – if available – lights flicker)*

Cop – It's happening!

Did. – *(A cabbage is thrown onto the stage. He catches it)* A new particle!

(More cabbages are thrown. One hits Big Bonus. His suitcase flies open and cabbages fall out. He turns to face audience holding his head which has turned into a cabbage.)

Big Bonus – Please, please, somebody bail me out please, please, a bailout, a bailout!

END

Graham Chadwick

Tempus Fugit Babe

His
A few years ago I could scare,
Zappata moustache and wild hair.
But now I am bald (a wide parting it's called)
I could do with a 'syrup' to wear.

Hers
I used to wear leggings and minis,
My friends and I were all skinnies.
Now we pig out on chips,
Have huge flabby hips,
Gorging chocolate, pizzas and tinnies.

Chris Davenport

In '87

We made love once
In Fawsley Park
On a balmy summer afternoon.

We'd turned our backs
On the narrow dusty lane
Choked with cars
Crawling like lazy ants,
And slipped gingerly
Through a barbed-wire fence
Into a field of sheep.

I led a zig-zag way,
Avoiding droppings and old cow-pats,
Until I found a patch,
Well-chewed, yet verdant green;
Unsoiled.

You squeezed my twitching hand,
Pulled me gently to the ground
And I lay beside you fumbling
With your long cotton dress.

Afterwards, I bobbed my head to see
If the walkers by the lake
Might have glimpsed anything
But the sheep were grazing
Contentedly between us and them.

We dozed in the shimmering stillness,
Quiescent, just fingers intertwined,
Until a dog barked, scattered the sheep,
And discovered us,
And I wondered what he could smell.

As we walked to the lake you told me
How one hundred years ago
To the week,
John Merrick, the Elephant Man,
Had come here to find refuge
From staring eyes and comments;
Seek solitude and harmony
In this isolated haven;
And I felt guilty that we had just shared
An intimacy here
That he had probably
Never, ever known.

Martin Rimmington

*Footnote: John Merrick visited and stayed at Fawsley Park,
Northamptonshire in 1887*

Time and Tide

The sheets release a warm scent of fresh air and daisies as they tumble out of the airing cupboard. Toby picks out a cover, two pillowcases and a sheet. Then he tries to push the rest back onto high slatted shelves, squeezing and shoving as hard as he can until, reluctantly, he leaves them heaped up on the carpet and pads back along the landing to his room.

As he enters dark shapes flicker like sharks across the blue wallpaper. He drops the bedding and tugs hard at the curtain cord. Early morning sunlight floods in, chasing the sinister shadows away. Scuba Action Man, propped up on Toby's bookshelf, is holding his harpoon at the ready. Toby raises his right hand and salutes. Now he can tackle the bed. He takes hold of the bottom end of his duvet and begins to undo the buttons one by one, counting in his head as he goes, tongue held firmly between his teeth in concentration.

Toby's mum has shown him how to do up buttons using a special cloth book that Grandma made for her when she was a little girl; Toby finds it hard to believe Mum was ever the same age as him. On each page of the book Grandma had sewn felt pictures using tiny stitches in matching thread, each designed to help his mum (and Uncle Alex after her) practise how to do and undo different fasteners. Mum said her favourite had been the blue poppered purse embroidered all over with pink nosed white rabbits. She added that Grandma, to encourage her, had sometimes hidden treats inside.

'A sixpence, and sometimes a toffee, if I was lucky.'

Toby wasn't sure what a sixpence was, but he liked the

idea of discovering a yummy toffee.

Last week he'd mastered the poppers, practising every night until the tips of his fingers tingled, relishing the 'click', as he centred the little silver bulb and pushed down hard. Then, on Friday bedtime, he'd found a golden disc of toffee inside a crisp five-pound note. Put it towards something special, Mum told him, when he ran downstairs to show her what he'd found. He'd folded the money over and over until it fitted through the slot of his Hamm piggy bank. It didn't make quite such a satisfying noise as the loose change Dad let him have when he'd topped the car up with petrol, but he knew it was more important, like the money that slid out of birthday cards.

After the poppers, he'd moved on to the next page of the book. Here Grandma had turned two pieces of bright blue felt into a smart waistcoat fastened with three shiny silver buttons – a tiny red silk triangle, for a handkerchief, peeking out of its pocket.

Toby pauses for a moment as he tries to remember what to do. Last night, before bed, Mum had sat beside him, arm warm against his, as she watched his efforts.

'Lift the button up, Toby, let it slide through the hole. Like when you post the letters for me in Morrisons.'

His fingers had fumbled as he tried to push the first one through the rigid mouth of the buttonhole. Then, after a few tries, it had slipped into place.

'Well done, Toby. See, practice makes perfect.' Mum patted his hand. 'You'll be on to tying up laces before you know it.'

Toby noticed Mum's eyes had gone all shiny. She smiled at him, dabbing at the corners of her eyes with her apron. He reached over and gave her one of his extra mighty hugs. Her apron still held the warm smell of apple crumble from teatime; he'd managed two ginormous helpings with custard. Grandma's recipe. And her book. Mum was probably thinking about her. On holiday Dad had explained to Toby that Mum was sometimes sad because Grandma wasn't there any more.

'Your mum still misses her. Mums are very important, even when you're grown up,' Dad said.

Toby understood. He'd been very sad when he'd accidentally left Limpet, his toy seal, behind at the service station near Bristol. Missing your mum must be much, much worse.

'Done it,' says Toby, as the last button comes free. He wiggles his aching fingers before trying to remove the cover. The duvet rucks up in peaks as he pulls, sticking to the cover like the Velcro tabs on his slippers: as one side comes free, the others creeps back on. The sun has moved round now, its hot tentacles stretching across the cotton rug and up the side of the bed. Toby sits for a moment to think, then throws off his dressing gown, mounts the bed and fights his way into the cover.

Inside, he crosses his legs and holds the cover up over his head. The light goes blurry and strange – a bit like being in Dad's old tent last summer, except this doesn't have squashed flies on it. Toby giggles at the memory. He'd loved snuggling up with Limpet in his new sleeping bag, listening to the other campers as they settled down for the night, and his parents' murmuring in the next compartment before he drifted off to sleep. And, in the morning, when the birds woke him with their chirruping, he would listen out for the swish of high tide pushing limpet shells and seaweed onto nearby Perranporth beach; after a breakfast of bacon and eggs from the farm he and Dad would forage for these treasures, gathering them up to decorate the sand

boats they spent every morning building.

Camping had been brilliant fun. And so, thinks Toby, is this. Outside on the close a car engine starts, revving as it pulls away. Toby listens, but the house is still quiet. He needs to get on. Holding the two far corners tight in his fists he emerges, hair sparking with static.

The elastic corners of the bottom sheet ping off one by one; Toby quickly peels off the two pillowcases and rolls the bedding into a ball. He can help do that later. His job is to hand Mum the pegs as she pins out Dad's shirts, Toby's playgroup clothes and her uniforms on the carousel. Afterwards, Toby likes to watch through the patio window, munching squashed fly biscuits with his milk as the washing bucks and twirls like white sea foam horses. On holiday, Dad pointed these out to Toby as they planted the Jolly Roger on the sand prow of their latest pirate ship.

'Choose one, Tobes, and we'll have a race.'

He and Dad had jumped and cheered each time the white manes of their wave horses rushed in. Then Toby had noticed the surfers zigzagging their way through the spray, wet hair clinging to their faces, bodies shiny in black rubber, boards flashing. They reached the shore faster than the horses, and Toby had stared and stared until his eyes smarted with salt.

Dad tapped him on the shoulder. 'Earth to Toby.'

'Look Dad,' said Toby, almost breathless with excitement, 'they beat both of us. I want to learn how to do that. Can I? Please.'

Dad put his hand on Toby's head, ruffling his hair. 'Maybe next year, Tobes. You need to be a pretty good swimmer first.'

That last night in the tent, sleeping bag zipped up to his chin against the cold, Toby had dreamed of skimming across the sea, slick as a seal, with the sea gulls swooping low, squawking their encouragement as they chased him in.

Toby heaves the last corner of the fitted sheet over the mattress. Its wrinkles remind him the backs of Grandma's hands. He can't remember much about her, as he was only two and a half when she died, and that was ages ago. Except for her hands. He'd loved watching her fingers loop strands of wool around fast clicking needles, magically transforming them into pieces of a jumper, or sending floury clouds into the air as she mixed and stirred in the kitchen with Mum. Toby would run his fingers over the ripples and speckles on her hands as she read to him. Each one held a story, Grandma had said. Maybe Mum missed Grandma's stories.

Toby abandons his task, leaving the sheet curled up like the edge of a Cornish pasty. Once the duvet is on no-one will notice, and anyway his feet don't reach that far down the bed. The twelve white discs slip into their buttonholes. Toby climbs up on the bed and shakes the duvet until it lies smooth; he places two pillows, one green, one red, at the head of the yellow and blue striped cover. Stepping back on the rug, he admires his handiwork, claps his hands in delight. His room is now full of sunshine and colour – just like the seaside. If only he was there now...

Toby rolls up his pyjama legs, heaves the oblong rug onto the bed. Spacing his feet out wide, one in front of the other to balance his weight, he braces his knees. Behind him the bedroom door opens.

'Wave coming,' he shouts, shifting his makeshift board to catch the surf, just as the Perranporth surfers had done. 'Ripper,' he whoops. He imagines Mum and Dad watching him in amazement from the shore, and he waves both arms in their direction.

Whump.

Toby finds himself tangled in a knot of bedding, gazing up at Mum's flowery dressing gown.

'I think that's what they call a wipe-out,' Mum says, hauling him to his feet. She glances round the room and her eyes widen. 'What have you been up to, Toby?'

'I did my bed, all nice an' tidy.' He looks at the mess. 'It's all spoilt now.' His eyes start to prickle, and he rubs furiously at his nose.

'Let me see now. Here, you take this.' His mum gathers up the crumpled duvet and pillows whilst Toby shakes out his rug.

'You have saved me a job this morning.' His mum nods at the tidied rainbow bed. 'And you managed to do all those buttons,' she says, smoothing the electricity out of his hair. 'Grandma would be so proud.'

'Can we go camping again this summer?' Toby asks, holding his breath and crossing his fingers.

'Would you like to?' Mum asks, hooking back the curtains.

'Yes please,' Toby answers quickly. 'At Perranporth.' He looks across to Action Man, whose scuba kit is neatly lined up next to him along the shelf. 'And can I have a wetsuit with a shark on it? And surfing lessons?'

'Let's go see what your dad thinks, shall we?' Mum smiles. 'Only first, we'll make him a cup of tea.' She takes Toby's hand and they head downstairs.

'And, Mum?

'Yes, Toby.'

'If I save up, can I buy my own surfboard?'

Claire Yates

Time Flies...

The smell was puzzling and increasing in strength. Lucy screwed up her nose in disgust as she moved past the pile of post, through the hall and into the kitchen. Outside, Daniel was still grappling the suitcases down from the roof-rack after their annual fortnight in Cornwall.

Lucy quickly flung open the back door and kitchen window, letting in a welcome breeze. She circled the kitchen, sniffing the air like a terrier, following the scent. She stopped at the freezer and tried not to gag at the overpowering stench. The absence of the green flashing light on the door confirmed her fears. Gingerly she pulled on the steel handle and retched as a cloud of bluebottles spilled out of the warm space, revealing their welcome home dinner – steak and maggots.

Anne Lawson

Cul de Sac

Late July, and the grey tarmac was melting. A fat girl
stole the cabbage white butterfly from my yellow bucket
and squashed it because she could.

Janet Lewison

Greetings from Scarborough

It's surprising sometimes what the old people bring with them into the Home. Of course, there's not a lot of space in a ready-furnished room. Once they've filled a couple of suitcases with the essentials – clothes, dressing gown, slippers and toiletries – the rest of their possessions have to be abandoned.

The family heirlooms go to the children; the antique sideboard moves in with a niece; a nephew takes the fireside chair; and the remains of their life's bric-a-brac - their cut glass, books, china dinner service, music and photos – is re-homed, shared out, sold on eBay or left with Oxfam.

But there's always a little something that they manage to bring in with them, almost subversively hidden in a pocket or tucked into a slipper, some insignificant-looking object concealed between the cardigans, a small piece of property that can, Tardis-like, open up worlds of memories for them in reduced surroundings.

For Molly it was a tiny china dog that sat on the top shelf next to her daughter's photograph. The dog's left ear was chipped, but its eyes seemed warm and it had a friendly face. It watched over her, so Molly said, cheered her up, reminded her of Charlie, running after balls, fetching sticks and chasing cats. She would giggle guiltily, remembering the time he almost caught the neighbour's rabbit.

Harold's memories lay in a row of medals, stashed away in a small cardboard box in the bedside drawer, whilst the jewellery box on Dorothy's dressing table concealed another world. The box was made of sandalwood, a present from her late husband from a business trip to Morocco many years ago. You could still smell the scent when the box was opened. She would ask me to pass it to her and she would fumble with arthritic fingers to lift the lid and sit, eyes closed, breathing sandalwood pictures into her mind, reliving moments from a younger, happier past.

But it was Albert's treasure that was the most surprising, for two reasons. Firstly, it was nothing more than an old picture postcard, black and white, with 'Greetings from Scarborough' printed jauntily across the top in curly lettering – not valuable, not exotic, not cute or cuddly, just a tatty old postcard. But the thing that was so intriguing – unexpected – was that it depicted a seaside landscape covered in snow. Every day I would see it as I tidied his room; the white path that snaked its way gently down from white cliffs to join a white promenade that led away towards a distant white sea-front. Only a lone gas lamp stood stark and black against the grey sky, bravely illuminating the wintry gloom, while a single set of childish footprints led along the promenade before disappearing round a corner, small black ovals in the empty whiteness.

The cheery greeting jarred uncomfortably with the bleak view.

It was unnerving.

Eventually, I could contain my curiosity no longer. I just had to ask Albert. Who had sent it to him? Why present such a dismal view? Wasn't it rather unusual to send a holiday postcard in winter – and from Scarborough? The more I thought about it, the stranger it seemed. Wasn't Scarborough a summer destination? Surely 'Greetings from Scarborough' should arrive warm, sun-kissed, tasting of salt and sand. For a start, it should be in

colour, with a dazzling blue sea unfolding its foaming spray along the shoreline. The beach should be a rainbow of striped deck-chairs bulging with babbling holiday-makers. I should almost hear the braying of a seaside donkey as I skimmed my duster along the window-ledge and flicked it over the tiny bookshelf, where the postcard was propped up against an old photograph album and a few well-thumbed crime novels.

Albert smiled from his armchair.

'Bring it here and sit down a minute, love,' he said, 'and I'll tell you. Here.' He patted what he jokingly called his visitor's chair, a shabby affair with no arms. He kept his stick hooked over the back and his newspaper on the faded seat. He liked to do the crossword every day. Kept his brain active, he said.

I moved the paper and sat down.

'Well?' I asked, handing him the card.

'You see them footprints?' he asked. 'Here, in the snow? Well, them's mine.' He grinned proudly.

'Yours?' I stared at him in disbelief.

'Me dad were a photographer,' Albert said. 'Had a studio in Scarborough and did portraits. It were all the rage then, 'specially with so many visitors in the summer. Did a roarin' trade.'

Albert looked down at the postcard in his hands and stroked it gently. 'But before that, before the portraits took off, he did picture postcards. Lovely views all round Scarborough where we used to live, and the east coast, from Filey all the way up to Whitby. He loved taking pictures. Used to experiment with views and angles and changing seasons. Liked to try to get summat a bit different.'

Albert paused and peered again at the wintry scene. 'I

were just a little lad when he took this, 'bout six or seven years old. There'd been a heavy fall of snow and he was keen to go out and take pictures. Me mam dressed me up warm and off we went down to the sea-front. There was no-one about, not a soul. We were the first down the cliff path and onto the prom. Dad told me to walk ahead of him and wait for him round the corner. Then he took this photo and had it made into one of his first ever postcards. Look, here's his name printed on the back.' Albert proudly handed me the card.

'That's lovely,' I said, taking it and turning it over and back, looking again at the child-sized footprints and then at the faded name of the keen, young photographer. 'Really lovely. Much better than an ordinary seaside postcard. Thanks, Albert.'

'You're welcome.' He smiled. ''Course, I made a pile of snowballs while I were waiting and pelted him with them when he came round the corner. Nearly got a good hiding for soaking his camera, but he saw the funny side. We spent the rest of the morning building a huge snow-man on the beach.' Albert settled back in his armchair, grinning. I could see him reliving the moment, taking his dad by surprise with a well-aimed lob and a flurry of snowflakes. In his mind he was six again, shrieking with laughter and bursting with mischief and energy.

'I'd better get on,' I said, reluctantly breaking the spell. 'No rest for the wicked! Sandra should be along with your tea soon.'

Albert nodded absently, still smiling, his mind else-where.

I popped the card back in its place.

'See you tomorrow, Albert.'

I've often wondered since what small thing I might

have to pack in my suitcase one day, what insignificant-looking memento would be able to capture so perfectly the Genie of my memories and keep them snug and safe until the moment of release?

The next morning, Matron met me as I signed in.

'It's sad news, I'm afraid, Jo,' she said. 'Albert passed away in the night. I know you were fond of him. I'm sorry.'

I must have looked such a sight, gawping like a fish in fresh air.

'But he was fine yesterday!' I said. 'We had such a chat...'

'I know, I know,' said Matron. 'It was a bit of a shock to us all. But he went peacefully in his sleep. And he's left you this.' She handed me an envelope with 'For Joanna,' written in proper ink in a rounded, old-fashioned hand.

I opened the envelope.

'Greetings from Scarborough' met my pricking eyes. Shakily, I pulled out the postcard. Through the blur, I saw the familiar white landscape, the gas lamp standing sentinel and the prom leading down towards the sea-front.

Then I noticed that the line of little black footprints had vanished under a fresh fall of snow.

Anne Lawson

3.33 to 3.43 p.m.

Scrawny thin and
Heavy-bellied mums
(Why only mums ?)
Guide creaking buggies
Behind their homebound treasures
Careering jauntily ahead;
(except some mums clasp
Their treasure hand-grip fast
Ignore the protest pleads –
'Not fair! Let go!')
And 'MIND THE DOG
DIRT, darling!' comes too late
As treads and threads of brown
Cling resistant – ugh! – to heels
And wheels along a track
One-way busy.

Martin Rimmington

Camping Clarity

Camping for me is a time to let go,
To reset my speed to comfortably slow,
Make time to explore, to wonder, to share,
To kick off my shoes and muss up my hair,
To leave off mascara, pull on warm socks,
Look to the stars, and ignore ticking clocks,
Turn off machines and throw on cagoules,
Muddle up mealtimes, put aside rules,
Listen to rain drops, sardonic ducks,
Tear up my lists and escape rumbling trucks.

To wade into rivers, make treasures of stones,
Admiring their beauty, their textures and tones,
To lie down in meadows, my energies spent,
Breathing in cowslips, their cognitive scent,
Peer into hedgerows, marvel at birds,
Join in their song and make up new words.

To have picnics on beaches whenever I like,
Stomp up a hill or freewheel on my bike.
For camping – read clarity
For limits – read free
Camping is down time, to pause, and just be.

Claire Yates

Months

January days crack corners crust
February folds in soft grey dusks
March swoops in with flowers in frost
April anchors winds of lust
May sings sweet her colours cast
June conceals a tongue held fast
July revolves in an open door
August lays us on the floor
September softens up our skin
And October ushers crisp leaves in
November dances in the sky
December! How the year did fly

Vicky Adshead

Silver Threads

APRIL

The forsythia splashes butter yellow across the wall, while early bulbs peek out of the soil and primroses make a welcome return to the borders.

The question of our Silver Wedding Anniversary comes up. Stephen suggests we celebrate with a cruise. Barry rejects the idea outright and mumbles something about a small 'do' and keeping it in the family. Seems a bit mean – after all, it will be 25 years of marriage. However...

MAY

I'm delighted to spot the blue irises as well as the white blossom which is weighing down the branches of the old tree near the shed, not to mention the biennial honesty. The latter is like an old friend. The days are certainly warming up.

It almost feels like old times when we sit down to Sunday lunch. It's the one time guaranteed to see the three of us together. I expect it's part of modern day life this snacking, eating on the hoof as they say. Even Barry rarely makes it home in time during the week to eat a meal with me and if Stephen is out with Annie, his girlfriend, I sit at the table alone.

JUNE

The ornamental rhubarb with its jagged leaves will die off quite early in the summer. By the end of the month we should see signs of the blue meadow cranesbill. I love the peppery scent of the lupins and their majestic spires.

Stephen is sitting his 'A' levels and studying very hard. Hope he gets the results he wants and goes to Durham. Mind you, what I'll do when he's gone I don't know. HE doesn't seem at all concerned about his son's future.

JULY

The voluptuous hydrangea is resplendent; it dwarfs the tufted blue vetch, but sets off the Japanese white anemones.

Stephen's left school now. He's off to stay in a friend's villa in France, somewhere near St. Malo I think. HE hasn't mentioned a holiday for just the two of us. He just suggested I go and stay with my sister, Maureen, in Falmouth for a week or so.

AUGUST

The lawn has greened up and is studded with yellow daisies. The flowering grasses in the far corner add a bizarre touch, waving to all and sundry when there is a breeze.

Stephen's got the results he wanted — three straight A's, so his place is assured. I'll soon be on my own. HE took a few days off whilst I was with Maureen. A fishing trip was mentioned in passing without any further details. Funny really, he's never shown any interest in the sport before.

SEPTEMBER

The verbena builds to a climax this month. Its tall square green stems make a greater impression than its small leaves. The fuchsias also look their best, especially the gorgeous blood-red ones.

Stephen has gone, so it's just me left. I no longer do any baking and the Sunday roast has become a thing of the past. There doesn't seem much point. HE's increased his workload and spends more and more time tucked away in his study on the increasingly rare occasions that he's at home.

OCTOBER

Hurrah for Michaelmas daisies and the red hot pokers, even if their season is only brief.

I mention the possibility of a short break, a weekend away, now that our son is at university. HE replies brusquely, indicating that he's much too busy at work. Most evenings I make the meal and leave it for him to pop in the microwave.

NOVEMBER

Shades of autumn are apparent. The pyracantha protects the remaining bushes from the enemy and provides a treat for hungry birds. Falling night temperatures. I put on the winter duvet.

HE has been away for two weekends this month. Business conferences I am informed. I am not given a contact number in case of emergencies. I eat off a plate in front of the TV. It's come to this!

DECEMBER

At least the ivies look good in winter and the first hellebores will be out by Christmas. The wood pigeons are feasting on clusters of orange berries.

HE is coming home later and later. Never mind, Stephen will be here soon to inject some life into the place. Perhaps things will be better when we're all together again, a family of three, enjoying a turkey with all the trimmings.

JANUARY

Tiny snowdrops are peeping through. Bare stems and leaf skeletons make an attractive picture when rimed and silvered with frost.

No New Year's resolutions made as yet. Stephen's gone back to uni. The house feels cold even with the heating turned up to maximum. HE fails to come home on two occasions. No reasons forthcoming. We've not sat down together since Christmas, not for a meal or a chat. Notes are left on the fridge door.

FEBRUARY

Short days and overcast skies. Thank heavens for the magnificent grey cut leaves of the cardoons. The witch-hazel bush is at its best, while the tulips are truly up and awake.

HE has taken up golf and is at the club every weekend. Well, at least a set of brand new clubs is loaded into the boot of his car. He hasn't spoken for days, although he has purchased yet another mobile. He sports a pungent aftershave and I catch sight of some minimal snazzy undergarment in place of his usual saggy Y-fronts.

MARCH

The dog's tooth violet has made its appearance along with the yellow Welsh poppies and giant bluebells. By the end of the month the native narcissus will come into its own. The season of re-birth is fast approaching with its exuberant spurt of regeneration, new life following the gloom of winter.

The golf clubs show no sign of use; the club has no knowledge of his membership.

The whole garden is bathed in moonlight making the white flowers glow and the silver leaves gleam. The effect is a magical one.

Stephen has called this evening. He's invited me up to Durham for the weekend and I've promised Maureen I'll pop down to Falmouth again before long. I wonder what April will bring.

Barbara Oldham

Growing Up In Another Time

Anthony Burgess wrote a book called The End of the World News, and today we have the end of the News of the World. My initial reaction is delight; an ugly, faded piece of tasteless, mindless, graffiti has been scrubbed off a wall. Then I recalled the time I used to be a regular reader in the late forties and early fifties. The News of the World was my sex education manual. It's difficult to imagine just how repressed – or protected – we were. Matters had hardly moved on since the boy Bertrand Russell had been chastised for using the word Virgin at the Victorian family dinner table. I remember being baffled one day when I was similarly corrected for muttering the word Sod.

My maternal grandmother must have been of a rather more liberal bent than her daughter, my mother, who somewhere along the line had gotten religion in a particularly claustrophobic form. Losing one husband in the Flanders mud and then having a second slowly going blind as a result of exposure to mustard gas had cured Grandma of any religion. And it was in my grandmother's home I read the News of the World and picked up the clues – and cues – which enabled me to go on to painfully piece together what was meant by that mysterious phrase, 'The Facts of Life'.

The paper's presentation of these things was in those days extremely coy, prurient and deeply hypocritical. In fact it seldom used the big word Sex at all and what are now called four letter words were undreamt of, even asterisks. The reporting was undoubtedly sensationalist but not yet to me. What is now known as The Sex Industry was called simply Vice and it was located exclusively in a place called Soho where ladies took off their clothes for men to see their naked bodies. That was all very bad but I wasn't sure why. I would have quite liked to see naked ladies too, but I wasn't sure why.

But it was the reporting of rape and divorce cases which was most informative because it contained verbatim evidence from witnesses although their testimonies were still heavily censored via cross examinations conducted in euphemisms. The key phrases, used time and time again, were 'You were intimate' and 'Intercourse took place.' In one dictionary I found 'intercourse' linked with 'sexual' and proudly introduced this new phrase, 'sexual intercourse', to a gang of male chums at school. They were unimpressed. All I was doing was giving them a couple of long words – and they were mostly much less literate than me – which meant what they called, 'doing it' and which didn't take us much further towards understanding what 'it' was. Of course they all pretended to know what 'it' was but in fact they knew very little and much of what they thought they knew was plain wrong. Their reluctance to admit their ignorance was the chief obstacle to enlightenment. Sometimes theories were aired. You did 'it' with a girl and then she had a baby. That was close but led to incredible ideas like babies actually growing inside and coming out of girls. That was, to us, science fiction and very frightening. This fear meant further ignorance and denial and was, I suppose, psychologically, quite damaging in the long run. But the News of the World seemed to back up such a preposterous theory. 'Intimacy' was sometimes followed by babies. Some boys had mothers who were having babies but often small brothers were not told anything until mum went away one day and came back the next with a new brother or sister no questions asked or answered. We were left to surreptitiously and guiltily put the pieces together ourselves; we noted that women were fat before they 'collected' their babies and less so afterwards, we spied on couples doing 'it' in the park and some of us joined the library. What we found out was exciting but repellent too. Of course those with sisters – and I didn't – had an advantage. Sisters would tell – and show, sisters learned from their mothers. Fathers told us nothing.

Some of us travelled well into puberty before we learned all the FACTS OF LIFE and, more significantly, accepted them. If only the News of the World had told it straight – that would have really been sensational.

Graham Chadwick

The 'Pina Colada' Girl

Monday

Dear Diary,
I am bored! BORED! Tired of the same old routine! Married for fifteen years and just look at us, where did it go so wrong? Life is so boring, I hate my job, I hate this town, I hate… Well no, I don't hate Josh, but look, he's been to the bathroom and brushed his teeth and now he's going to fold his dressing gown, get into bed and then start reading the paper. Oh, I forgot, first he comes across to give me a goodnight peck on the cheek. Where did all the passion go, the excitement, the raised pulse, the somersault in my tummy? We don't even sleep in the same bed any more; I know that moving into the spare room was my idea while we had our bedroom decorated, but that was six months ago and we still show no signs of wanting to move back.

Tuesday

Dear Diary,
Boring work again, though at least we all had a laugh at lunch time today, talking about men, what else? Melanie, in accounts, says she thinks Josh must be having an affair. According to her you can always tell when a man is seeing another woman: he becomes distant, distracted. I say this sounds familiar – just yesterday Josh forgot to pick up his suit from the dry cleaner's and then blamed me, claiming I'd lost his ticket. Honestly! Men! Melanie thinks I need to have an affair too, bring some thrills back into my life: it will make me appear more interesting, was how she put it. I said that's all very well, Melanie, but where am I going

to meet someone? Val from the footwear department then told us all about her experiences with the dating agency she's been trying. Val's been divorced for about ten years and hasn't had a real relationship since. The men she dates either don't call her again or else bring their kids along on the second date. Still, like she says she hasn't yet met a George Clooney lookalike, so she keeps trying. My friend Jan thinks I should put an ad in the personal column, so I'm working on that. I'll tell you all about it tomorrow.

Wednesday

Dear Diary,

I've been doing some research on the personal ads and found there's quite an art to writing a good one. For a start it took me quite a while to crack the codes. WLTM – ah yes, *would like to meet.* And how about this one – GSOH or even VGSOH? Yes I know now – *good sense of humour,* etcetera. Do they mean they won't be too depressed even though they're going through a bitter divorce, I wonder? And then how do you describe yourself in just a few lines? I think it must be a bit like selling a house; no way do you recognise it as yours when you read the estate agent's blurb. Think I'll just cut through all that gobbledygook and get straight to the chase.

Dear Diary, did I mention I am having a nightcap while I write this? Very decadent, a glass of red wine in bed! Josh is away at some conference or other (see, I told you, Melanie will say). By the way, did I tell you what Sally from perfume said the other day? She reckoned you can tell a lot about a person by what they drink. So how about, 'I'm a girl who likes cocktails'? Does it make me sound sophisticated and chic? That reminds me of the time I went on a buying trip to London with Susie from lingerie. In the evening we went into the hotel bar to chill out and after a couple of red wines I was up for a spot of flirting with the French barman. Susie dared me to ask him for that saucy cocktail 'Sex on the Beach' so I went over to the bar and... chickened out! I couldn't, I was blushing for a start! Instead, I asked for the first drink I could think of, which was 'Pina Colada'. I don't think I've ever had it since, so that could be my own secret code. That's what I'll write: 'Do you like Pina Coladas?' Yes! I come across as being sophisticated, and acquire a Caribbean laid back approach to life in just two words.

– Okay Diary, how about the next line? How do I sound like the free spirit I really am inside without coming across as a bit of a fruitcake? Ok, I love the simple things in life, those things that are free, so I'll just go with that. How about: 'I love walking in all weathers and don't mind getting caught in the rain.' Ha, ha, I adore being out during a thunderstorm, it's always a good excuse to take wet clothes off and snuggle up to get warm. I remember how Josh and I got caught out like that once when we were courting. Health and safety would probably put a stop to that too if they could, 'not good for the health of the nation, overloading our care services, etcetera, etcetera.' And while I'm on the subject, I'm fed up with being told 'eat this, don't drink that, exercise more.' Isn't it time we took responsibility for our own diet and lifestyle? I don't want to be super thin with arms like sticks thanks to personal trainers and power yoga, that sort of thing. Down with political correctness, I say! I want to break free! And I want a man with a brain who feels the same way. Oh, and sex on the beach. Okay, okay, I'll tone it down a bit. How does: 'making love at midnight down by the dunes' sound? Dear Diary, will I get that line past the censors, do you think?

Thursday

Dear Diary,
Well, I did it – I sent it off. I daren't look to see if it is in tonight's edition. Josh is back from his business trip and is reading the paper right now. I think I'll pretend to be asleep.

Friday

Dear Diary,
You'll never guess! I got a reply and he's made me laugh before we even met, how about that? (GR8SOH!) He said he is most positively not into health food, and always thought that tofu and quark were something to do with quantum physics. He loves walking, though not tramping over moors: strolls by the ocean in the moonlight are more his thing. He says he's not sure about 'Pina Colada', unless he can count it as two of his five-a-day, but even then thinks he still prefers champagne. Like I said – my kind of guy.

I could hardly wait to meet him, so when he suggested Harry's bar after work I agreed like a shot. I walked in and – well – there he was. I saw his broad shoulders and when he turned to me and smiled my heart did a little flip. I had to work fast though, as a predatory blonde was already eyeing him up. So I walked over and put my arm through his and gave him a big wink. 'Hi darling Josh,' I said, 'let's grab that bottle of champagne and escape to the beach.'

That was earlier, much, much earlier. He said he never knew I liked all those things so we had a lot of talking to do, oh, and other things. We're back in the double bed and newspapers are banned. I'm sorry, but there's no more time to write now – here comes Josh back from the bathroom and he's heading this way, so goodnight dear, dear Diary.

Pam Hunter

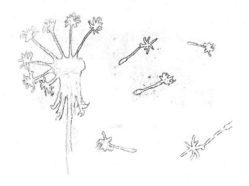

Cycling Ken

His rain-washed timber limbs wear canvas sails
Which catch at currents yawing down grey hills
And carry him past bleary shuttered shops,
Past stranded lifeless hulks of masted mills.

Both pedals spin like fish lures on the flat,
Slow, catching as he inclines towards the moor
Beneath him houses spread in building waves,
And roads cast lines around their urban shore.

Past idling fields he races round the lanes,
'Ahoy-ing' to the runners puffing by,
His winnowed hair swirling on the tide,
Unblustered by the steady dripping sky.

He bounces, buoyant, over cobbled streets,
By terraces blushing behind mended nets,
Sails through a shoal of babbling boys
Threading balls across the rippled setts.

A dome of emerald sparkles in his sights,
Its minaret, a peak of golden sun.
He tacks and turns his steady wheel to home,
Leans with the wind to ease the run.

Claire Yates

Barcarolle

As time laps gently on the stones
Whale aeons have rocked in the deep,
Horse-shoe crabs have come and gone
And returned again on a moonlit night,
Crept up the sucking shingle
To the soft dry dunes.

While out in the deep
The depravation of lone seamen,
Battling with the elements,
Finds no response in the plummeting waves.
No sense that here life had begun
And was one day quietly washed up.

At my feet the waves lap,
Softly surging in my ear,
Filling the night with meaning,
Soothing lone wanderers on the shore,
More newly born but more alone
Than the ghostly crabs
That move slowly on and on.

Robert Smith

'Night, Night'

Now Phoebe, you mustn't be afraid. Dark is just the light turned out. Look, I'll show you. I'll switch off my Barbie lamp. But I'll leave the door open. The landing light's on, so we can still see. No, it's not spooky. There's nothing to be scared of. I know, just so we won't feel alone, I'll have Giraffe with me and you can have Teddy. And, shall I tell you a bedtime story? What about Cinderella? No, that's not a scary one... night, night Phoebe.

Tonight Phoebe we're going to do the same as last night, only we'll close the door... no, not right to. I'll leave a gap so there's still light coming in. Shall we swap over and you have Giraffe and I'll have Teddy? That's not too bad is it? It's not really very dark is it? Shall I tell you a fairy story? Yes, it's a happy-ever-after one... night, night, hope the bugs don't bite. No, it's just something Mummy says when I'm in bed.

Mummy says that we're two brave little girls and Daddy says he's proud of us. You see, Phoebe, I have to do this before we go on holiday. I'm not sure why. It's something to do with not 'sturbing other people with lights left on. I don't really understand but I know that it's very important. What are we going to do tonight? The same as last night I think. No, Phoebe, you didn't hear a noise on the stairs. It's all right, I won't close the door right to. Not tonight. Whose turn is it for Teddy...? You want the story of Billy Bunny Rabbit again? Once upon a time... night, night.

It's only a shadow Phoebe. You know, it's something that happens when there's light and dark. Oh, and in the sun as well. Don't you remember last summer when we played that game chasing each other's shadow? No, I can't explain it, but it won't hurt us. Promise. Yes, I'll leave the door open a little. It's gone now. See, I told you there was nothing to be afraid of. Shall we have the story of the Gruffalo again? Not the bit where... all right, just the nice bit. Do you want Giraffe and Teddy tonight? Yes, you can have them both. I don't need them any more, I'm going to be brave and sleep without them. But I'll look after you – don't worry... night, night, sweet dreams.

Mummy says I've nearly reached my target. I didn't know what she meant until she explained. I must try to do without any light before my birthday. Shall we have one of Roald Dahl's stories tonight? A funny one? The Twits? I'm tired now... night, night Phoebe.

Daddy thinks that I can manage with my bedroom door closed all night now. He calls me his 'brave little girl'. I'll tell you one of my own stories tonight, one I made up... night, night.

I'm going to do it tonight. I've not had Barbie switched on for more than a month. I don't need her. Mummy's asked me if I'm ready to hit my target. I know what it means now. And, I'm going to show her that I can do it. I'm not frightened of the dark now, not even when I hear a noise. Sorry Phoebe, but I'm not telling you a story tonight... oh, I nearly forgot... night, night.

Phoebe, I've done it. Mummy and Daddy are very pleased. They're taking me to McDonald's for a 'Happy Meal' as a reward for trying so hard. I couldn't have done it without you. But, Phoebe, there's another thing, Mummy and Daddy have both said that they think I'm getting a little bit old to have you as a friend and that when we go on holiday you won't be able to come. They've told me that I will probably have some real friends to play with. I'll never forget you though and hope that you won't be afraid of the dark any more, just like me… goodnight Phoebe.

Barbara Oldham

A Week in the Life of a Teenager

SATURDAY

I feel my body shake, my head nod. I have a sensation of falling. I see pills around scattered like dandruff. I hear my mum sobbing: 'Why, oh why? No, now, it's an emergency.'

Sirens sound, lights flash. Jasper's whimpering in the corner. I am stretchered into oblivion…

FRIDAY

Poster up in school offering 'confidential' support group for others like myself. It's too late! New policy announced – DO NOT BLAME, DO NOT PUNISH **THEM!** Don't make me laugh. What about me? No blame! Everywhere I've gone they've been there – taunting, teasing, threatening: 'You're dead! – We're going to make your life hell!' Jasper's nearly drowned in all my tears.

THURSDAY

Mr Simons wants to see me – to do with my English course-work I suppose. I'd done it on time, but they took it, tore it into pieces. He'd never believe me if I told him the truth. Jenny scuttled away when she saw me in the corridor. She was my last hope. I used to be able to tell her how I felt. They've taken everything from me. There's nobody left except Jasper.

WEDNESDAY

They're in my face right from nine o'clock, following me everywhere. Waiting for me even though we're not in the same sets. Wonder who told them I got 92% in the maths test? Paid for it of course; this time it was physical. I'll have to tell mum I got hit in the hockey practice. Thank God for close contact sports. Sticks and balls have covered for several of my so-called injuries and when my blazer was covered in mud. Difficult explaining why I was wearing it during games. I hate lying to mum but she'd do something that would make it worse. What could she do? Wish I could ring her now – my mobile phone went weeks ago. I daren't tell her. Whisper in Jasper's ear how much the bruises hurt.

TUESDAY

Manage it as far as the school without incident. They lay into me about how I get others into trouble by handing in assignments on time. 'Creep,' they say. Time was when Jenny would back me up, but they got at her too. Threatened if she was seen hanging out with me she'd be for it as well. I don't blame her. Lasagne and salad for lunch, but I wasn't hungry. Jasper wags his tail when I get home.

MONDAY

Leave early in case they're waiting for me. It's never in public. Always round corners, dark places, the toilets. Pressure's on. It's money again. Why am I so weak? I can't say 'no,' I hand over the tenner gran gave me yesterday and a surge of hatred wracks my body. I feel sick but I daren't risk the toilets. I've only got enough left for lunch and the bus fare home. If they knew, they'd take that as well. Praised for handing in my completed art work on time – felt the daggers of hatred from **THEM!** Oh Jasper, why do they pick on me?

SUNDAY

Lie in. Get up around noon. Half the day gone. Where? Nearer to purgatory. Only 21 hours to go and it starts again. Will it ever end?

Is it my fault? Too fat? Too thin? Not attractive enough? Do I bring it on myself? Gran comes to eat with us. Jasper is the only one that I can talk to. Feed him some roast beef. He looks up gratefully. Trouble is, he can't help me. He can listen though. Watch half an hour of telly. Pretend to go up for an early night. Finish my history course-work for tomorrow and the art project. What's the point of imitating Van Gogh's style? What's the point period?

Barbara Oldham

Winter's Child

There is something special about this time of year when the low winter sun appears almost spiritual. The subtle colours of the skies and the quality of the light on days like these give a clarity that resonates within the mind. The trees are bare now, making their structure visible and more impressive; those things that were hidden, the birds' nests high in the branches and the beauty of the very few last leaves are now revealed. I have always considered myself to be a child of winter. For me, the heady profusion of reds and golds of the fall have always seemed too showy and gaudy: I prefer the ascetic, the Spartan, the frugal. Give me the restricted palette of winter, a monochrome world sparse yet powerful, and I can rejoice.

Into this meagre world comes the festival of Christmas, the pagan Yule: a surfeit to counter the shortage, a feast to defy the famine. And what a banquet it must have been in days gone by, when a whole community would sit down to dine. A whole roast pig or hog would usually be the centrepiece of the feast, and even today we still honour this tradition with pork or ham. Game birds would be plentiful, roast duck, capon and goose, as well as savoury pies or terrines of pheasant, partridge or pigeon, all eaten with stuffings of forcemeat, herbs and vegetables. Then came the sweetmeats: puddings and tarts made with dried fruits, apples and plums, plus jellies, junkets, creams and trifles. In addition, there would be indulgence and revelry with home brewed ales and ciders, and everyone would make merry.

When I was a child, on every Christmas Eve – that special time of waiting – mother used to make a savoury minced meat pie that was part of our own precious ritual; I used to love that pie as much if not more than the Christmas dinner itself.

Pam Hunter

Snow Fell (March 31st 1990)

Snow fell. Mewling cries and
Milk blue eyes saw you into our world.
Crib cosy you dozed.
We stood speechless as you sucked in air.

You knew your place. Central. Strong.
Dancing a glorious path as you grew,
Clinging on with simian strength
To knowledge, and our love.

Walls crumbled as you passed,
Lights flickered, dull and dark
Against your glow, your heat—
It warms us all.

Reluctant, we let you go.
You gather speed for take off, breathing fast.
Reaching. Determined. High.
We stand speechless, watching you climb.

Claire Yates

Close of Day, Winter

The clear light from a winter's afternoon drains inexorably westwards, as though a giant hand has pulled the plug on day. Trees on the far banks of the lake begin to withdraw as one into the dusk of the surrounding hillside, but not until the water's glassy surface has captured each outline, freezing each one for a heartbeat, before drowning all in an inky black watercolour of unfathomable depth.

Overhead, the skies shimmer in crystal and a brilliance of blues; flowing westwards, like a celestial glacier, the sunlight melts into the horizon, a dazzling finale of diamond yellow, haloing the distant hills; cold aquamarine sparkles above the lake; and deepening almost imperceptibly towards the east, evening hangs for a moment in triumphant turquoise before dimming to darkest sapphire.

In the stark branches of a solitary tree birds settle beneath the promise of a navy night, hushed and still.

As the earth turns its sleepy face with a satisfied sigh towards the darkening east, the last caress of light evaporates. The dampening ground exhales frail whispers of breath that gather and hang in pearlescent pools at the water's edge, shivering in anticipation of a frosty moon.

Anne Lawson

In Memoriam: May 2006

You didn't need a hearse, we lived too close by the cemetery,
And in any case, you rehearsed the moment every day,
From August, month of the *coup de foudre*, when
We fell in love again, and, as the Metaphysicals would have it,
Rolled ourselves, our lives, our love, into one ball,

A carnival balloon.

And when the past came knocking on the door
We made him leave his baggage in the street,
And saw off – pronto! – hawkers weighted down with phoney,
Bespoke, rehearsed grief - or miracles - or faith -
Faith which demands blindness when we most need our eyes,
And all our other senses too. No thanks!
Tomorrow never came, or if it did, slipped past us quick,
Stumbling backwards in a fog. Time can be still,
Like your photo on the wall;
You, racing in the Great North Run.
You said modestly, 'You can have my medals,'
I said, 'I didn't know,' nor did I know,
So much I didn't know.

From August until… no matter…
What matters is not time, or tenses,
But when you went on climbing, all those steps up to the
    Sacré Coeur,
The Eiffel Tower, spurning the *ascenseur* in *Printemps*,
Spurning your oxygen in your cheveril-gloved tops models gear,
And throwing-up on New Year's Eve – 'What else is new?'
    you smiled.

88

You took Death in your stride,
Running, but not top gear, not your top gear,
So I could keep up, jogging at your side.

That marble tomb you ordered – 'Retail therapy' –
It is a double bed, you've gone up early, left me to T.V.,
Keeping it warm, '*à demain mon mari, bonne nuit!*'

Graham Chadwick

Eternity

E ternity… what does this word really mean ?
T ime immemorial; in perpetuity; no dead 'has been'.
E ons, epochs, eras: each endures,
R eaches back and forth, somehow secures
N otions non-chronological, ideas of age abstract,
I nfinity, unprovable, yet definitely fact,
T he subject, Socratic onwards, on which men philosophise,
Y et for explanation perhaps probe deep beyond the skies.

Martin Rimmington

Dead leaves grind to dust
Mingle, change to earthy loam
Worms process, turning.

Claire Yates

The Months

(With apologies to Sara Coleridge)

A children's classic gets a cynical, adult makeover. By the way, there really is a wild flower called bloody cranesbill, but it's actually its cousin, Herb Robert, that's more likely to be a ****** nuisance to gardeners.

January pelts us with snow,
　Dig the car out and push if you've somewhere to go.

February lashes us daily with driving rains,
　'Til we're knee deep in slush with blocked up drains.

March flings breezes, bone numbing chills,
　Vandals have massacred the daffodils.

Still, April brings the primrose sweet,
　And spiteful showers of hail and sleet.

May gives us flocks of pretty little lambs,
　Displayed in the butchers' with sausages and hams.

June throws up dandelions, buttercups, bloody cranesbill.
　Scrub the moss off the patio, then spray down with weed kill.

July's jet stream mocks us with thundery showers,
　Causing torrential downpours for hours and hours.

But then August ripens the sheaves of wheat,
　Promising one day of summer, our annual treat.

In misty September we bring home the fruit,
If the harvest hasn't rotted both tree and root.

October is blighted with fog and pheasant shoots,
So turn up the heating and break out the booze.

Grim November gives us sad disease, as with icy blast,
The nights start drawing in thick and fast.

By arctic December, we're at the end of our tether,
Let's jet off abroad for some decent weather.

Pam Hunter

Every Second Counts

1.24 p.m. and 29 seconds. Paul snaps the pocket watch shut and feels his stomach shift again. Just over five minutes and his torment should end.

Five more minutes.

Five.

Tendrils of pain from knotted shoulders creep up and around his throat. He rolls his head from side to side attempting to loosen their grip. He tries to swallow, mouth desert-dry.

Through the pulsing blood in his ears, he thinks he can catch the faint notes of a piano, but the more he strains to listen, the more the silence roars, obliterating all sound.

He opens the case of the watch again and stares. The hands haven't moved.

For a second, he wonders whether the watch has stopped and for one glorious moment he dares to hope that time is already up and the agony over. But even as relief surges through his body, the rogue second hand that has hung back jerks forwards and advances around the watch-face in tiny, staccato steps.

Paul forces himself up from his seat, crosses the tired carpet and pretends to study the view from the dingy window. A depressing brick wall stares back at him. He can't pretend to admire a wall.

Returning to his seat, he glances again at the watch; the ordeal is nearly over. One minute left.

He coughs; drums impatient fingers on thigh; brushes away a speck of dust.

Suddenly the door bursts open and a small boy hurtles

towards him, clutching a music book.
      'I've passed, Daddy! I've passed!'

Anne Lawson

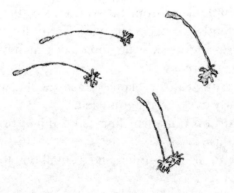

How The Body Came To Its Senses

Time didn't begin until the coming of mankind, as there was no-one to mark it. And right back then, at the beginning, with the world itself still in a state of flux, the human body wasn't as fixed as we know it now. Parts could be taken out or discarded, like the sixth sense, the loss of which we still feel to this day. Also some organs took time to perfect. For instance the eye, now regarded as a miracle of evolution, was once considered quite rudimentary, a fact which Sight soon forgot, so strongly did it believe itself to be the most senior, the king of all the senses. In fact, so competitive did the senses become, each vying to demonstrate that they alone were the one sense the body couldn't function without, that one day a quarrel broke out, a battle for supremacy which threatened to engulf the whole equilibrium of life. So, to settle the argument once and for all, it was decided that each sensory organ would take a year's break to wander the world alone, to see how the body could manage without them.

Sight reluctantly agreed to leave first, though he couldn't bring himself to go very far, being sure that he would soon be called back to take command of all the other senses. So he wandered about aimlessly, never far from home, keeping an eye on the place, all the time expecting to see the signal to return. But when he finally realised that none was going to come, he left and crossed oceans and deserts, seeing all manner of strange and exciting phenomena. The world of course looked very different back then, with no skyscrapers, no cars and no electricity, and the Milky Way hadn't yet been lost.

So it was that Sight travelled on in a state of heightened awareness, unencumbered by any other feeling and was able to see the world anew, as if for the first time, and this gave him far greater humility. But a year is a long time to be alone, and although he knew that he would never tire of seeing the glories of a rainbow sky at sunset or that first sight of a wisp of a new moon glowing brightly in the heavens, he discovered that he also missed the familiar sights of home and looked forward to the return. So, on the appointed day, a little unsure of his welcome and not a little worried about the welfare of the body after a year's absence, Sight returned and was joyously received.

'It's true that at first we missed you,' said the head, acting as spokesperson, when the welcome greetings had faded and Sight had told his story. 'Everything became instantly dark and we felt lost; simple pleasures like reading or writing were impossible. But we all pulled together and soon began to adjust. Fingers and hands became highly sensitive and in next to no time became skilled at distinguishing objects; the ears too worked extra hard to warn of any danger. We missed seeing the faces of our loved ones and the colours of the seasons but, by using our memory and imagination, and by looking through our mind's eye, we found we could visualise them and were content. And there were other compensations.'

'For a start, we couldn't see your great ugly feet,' joked the mouth.

'True', continued the head, 'but we also began to perceive and rely on the extraordinary kindness of strangers, the world seemed a gentler, more caring place.'

Next day it was the turn of Hearing to take his year's sabbatical. He called out a last goodbye, but when no answer came he went on his way. Now Hearing believed he had long been undervalued and unappreciated by the rest of the body, and dreamed of travelling the world alone to seek out and enjoy the most ravishing music. 'Ah, music,' he pondered. 'Was there anything ever created by man with a more powerful hold on our imaginations, with the ability to draw us in and hold us spellbound?' He was excited by the prospect of encounters with all manner of exotic musical instruments like the sitar, the balalaika, or zither, never ceasing to marvel at the ingenuity of human invention, for it seemed that nothing that was capable of making any kind of noise was ever overlooked in the quest to make the joyful, life affirming music which seemed to burst spontaneously into glorious reality.

Though music seemed truly to be a gift from the gods, Hearing also found the time to take pleasure in listening more acutely to the sound of the earth and the oceans, the calls of animals and birdsong. He also realised by the end of the year that there was no sound more beautiful than the voices of family and friends, and the laughter of children, and so he gladly returned.

The body then took up the story of its year without Hearing. 'It was very difficult at first,' said the head, 'for we were plunged into a silence so acute it was like living at the bottom of the deep ocean or the dark side of the moon. We had great problems trying to understand what people were saying and when, a little time later, Voice, who had been pining away, left us too, it became even harder.'

'It wasn't that,' said Voice, who had just at that moment returned, 'but since I could no longer hear my sound I had begun to wonder if I actually existed, so I too decided to take a gap year to try and find myself.'

'Well anyway,' the head continued, 'that didn't help

the rest of us, for we struggled even more to make ourselves understood. Being among strangers was especially difficult and frustrating and we were often treated like fools. Without our hands and eyes we would have felt isolated, but they rose to the challenge and learned to do our listening and talking for us; in fact we'll probably have a job shutting them up now. We realise now how important you are to our wellbeing and will never take you for granted again.'

Now Taste and Smell were practically inseparable, so they decided to go travelling together.

'And it's a good job we did,' said Taste on their return. 'You've all lost so much weight that we scarcely recognised you.'

'Thank goodness you are back,' said the body at their welcome home banquet. 'We have never spent such a miserable time. Food gave us no pleasure – in fact we have had to learn to eat to live rather than live to eat. But it wasn't just that, for we are surely more than just a physical body and being apart from you has helped us to realise that it's things like the scent of a pine forest or the taste of salt sea tang that enable us to conjure up involuntary memories, those moments of time that nourish our soul and console us.'

'It's true that most of my best memories are of meals shared with family and friends,' rumbled Belly, which made everybody laugh.

Touch, whose turn was next, had been very apprehensive about leaving. In fact, she couldn't imagine existing without the body and wanted to be allowed to go for just one day. But the body was eager to see how it would cope and so Touch had to go. At first she felt lost and drifted about quite aimlessly, feeling random things, like the cool softness of flowing water, or the different temperatures of smooth, hot metal. But as she got more into her stride she found that she had a precious talent for feeling the most minute imperfections in things like paper and fabrics, at the same time luxuriating in their soft sensuality.

However it was in the realm of the arts that Touch really excelled, and her work soon became much sought after. In drawing, her lines were praised for their sureness, as were her sculptures for their sensitivity of touch, and she played the piano with such a delicacy of touch that audiences were enraptured. In fact, she became so engrossed in this inner life that she lost all track of time, nearly missing the agreed deadline, for the year, moving ever more swiftly, had taken its course. It was time to return home.

Touch allowed sensation to return gradually, afraid that the shock of a sudden return might kill the body, so changed it was scarcely recognisable.

'Thank goodness you are back,' said the body. 'We haven't been able to function at all without you. Being unable to feel our limbs has meant that we couldn't walk, or hold anything, or even feed ourselves. Locked inside this body, totally dependent on others to look after all our daily needs has been deeply mortifying with only the eyes seeming to show life. We haven't even been able to gain comfort from the touch of others and with no physical contact at all with any living creature, it has seemed like the longest year of our life.'

And so, with the return of Touch, the senses began to work in harmony again – but still the body had one more idea, and a few days later called a meeting.

'Now,' said the body, when everyone was settled, 'it is Breath's turn to leave us.'

As Breath had taken no part in the original quarrel, merely going about its work, it was shocked and cried, 'I cannot leave you!'

The body laughed. 'We have all thought we were indispensable,' he said, 'but we have pulled through.'

'You could not survive for a year without me, though,' continued Breath. 'Why, you couldn't last for a day, or an hour; without me you would struggle to keep going even for a minute.'

'Why not go now?' the head insisted. 'We're sure we can manage.'

But still Breath found it hard to go, it was so deeply committed to the steady rhythm, to working even when the body and all its parts were sleeping. But the glimpse of freedom and chance to return to pure air spurred it on and with one huge effort it broke free.

As predicted, within a minute the body began to labour. Great gasping sobs were attempted but nothing could relieve it. Sight and Hearing had departed soon after Breath, and when Feeling too was lost the body gave out and fell. With one final superhuman effort the head managed to summon his last reserves of strength and gave an almost inaudible plea. 'Breath, please don't leave us,' he gasped.

So, Breath, who hadn't ventured too far, relented and leapt back into the body just in the nick of time. 'We were wrong,' the body admitted when it had recovered and got its breath back. 'We know now that you alone are essential to us, and that we cannot live without you. If you agree to stay we shall cherish and serve you all the days of our life.'

And so that is the story of how the body finally came to its senses. It was only in extreme old age when the memory of those early years had faded and the senses failed and left the body one by one, never to return, that Breath felt able to slip away and return to nature. And that is where you'll find it still to this day, if you only search.

Pam Hunter

Monday to Friday

6.42 MOVE INTO POSITION, ALIGN WITH DOORS. DUCK TO AVOID DEATH BY UMBRELLA SPOKES. BRIEFCASE – CHECK. TICKET – CHECK. MOUNT TRAIN. MAKE BEELINE FOR WINDOW SEAT WITH SOCKET. BINGO!

Claire Yates

Huck Finn

Barefoot, my brother and I bickered over becoming Huck Finn. Bravely we climbed the hot garage roof, sailed down the Mississippi and spat.

Janet Lewison

Darren's Downfall

(with acknowledgement to Hilaire Belloc)

When Darren was a little mite
He loved his food, slept through the night,
Smiled and giggled, read out loud,
All things to make his mother proud.
A mother's joy, a model child
Whom, adolescence had turned wild.
He turned into a hateful boy
Whose antics served most to annoy,
From turning cupboards inside out
To gouging out the bathroom grout
With toenail clippers – fancy that!
He ruined things, the little brat.
'Why did you do it?' Mum implored
As Darren vandalised, when bored,
His bedroom contents with a dart;
It fairly broke his mother's heart.
At mealtimes, when she called him down,
He'd skulk in, with a dreadful frown,
Eat greedily and creep away,
This happened every single day.
No 'please' or 'thank you' ever heard,
No gratitude, no, not one word.
He'd put on headphones, up the bass,
Then slam the front door in her face.

That day, his mother, home from work,
Found the door had gained a quirk:
Darren's constant jarring thrust

Had caused the hinge pins all to bust.
She rang the chap from Ease-Your-Lock
(*Opening hours: around the clock*)
He took the door off, shook his head
'New door and fittings here,' he said.
Mum paid the fee and waved goodbye,
'Good job I had a bit put by.'
Now safely in, she cooked her tea,
Then spying Darren's headphones free
She seized the chance for relaxation
And tuned into her favourite station.
The sofa, oh, so warm and cosy
Lulled her into feeling dozy.
She dreamt of children, neatly dressed
Who always, always tried their best.

Out late, our Darren felt the cold
But high on crack and feeling bold
He eyed up houses, calculating
Contents values, inside, waiting
To fill his pockets, pay for drugs
'Serves them right, the silly mugs.
No chains, alarms, or window locks,
This stealing lark – it really rocks.'

He scaled the fence, thought 'piece of piss,
A kid of two could manage this.'
When lights blazed on, a siren howled
And right behind him, something growled.
The dog pounced fast, its teeth snapped shut,
Drawing blood from Darren's butt.
He squealed with pain, then turned and ran,
Skidding past the coppers' van.

The night sky, thick with falling snow,
Made Darren's progress hard and slow.

Back at home he tried his key,
Then bashed the woodwork with one knee.
He shouted out, he stamped, he swore,
Then pounded on the altered door.
'It's Darren, open up, right now
And let me in, you stupid cow.'
Nothing stirred: no lights, no mum
So Darren slumped (ouch) on his bum
And shivered in his beanie hat,
His sole companion, next door's cat,
Who stared at him with utter scorn
Until it left to hunt at dawn.

Next morning, rested, light of heart,
His mother rose to make a start.
Then, finding that the milk was low,
She stepped outside, and stubbed her toe.

She looked down, sensing something horrid
And found her Darren, frozen solid.

Claire Yates

Extract from Tim Bobbin's Travels

Once more I and my bestiary escaped by getting ourselves swallowed by the whale and transported a thousand miles before she farted us out into the mouth of a shitty little creek called Port Mackeville in Queensland, Australia, (PMQ) There we had lashings of grass for the sheep and cows, sweet and sour prickly bushes for our goats and the endless BBQ trash made PMQ a paradise for our swelling company of rodents. Only Hogarth, the great white girlie pig, had reservations. She sniffed the air in her sniffy way and said it sniffed of fried fish and cheap gin like Blackpool. My mate, Blackamoor Coal, the runaway slave, seemed happy enough. He joined the Mackeville Amateur Dramatic Society (MADS) and took lodgings with a Scotch couple who claimed to be descended from the town's founding fathers – a claim disputed by the Italians who ran the local Amateur Operatic Society (MAOS). The Scotch Macks were horticulturalists who had succeeded in breeding a tartan rose which was PMQ's chief export.

The town had a motto painted on its welcome sign which was set curiously side-on to the road and easy to miss:

WELCOME TO PORT MACKEVILLE
– HERE TIME STANDS STILL
(Drive Carefully. Beware Roos)

One day I spied an aged man sitting on a fence by this sign and said the first thing to come into my head, 'I'm from Lancashire, been away a long time.'

'Time's relative,' he replied, 'like the sign says, when it's standing still there's no time at all.' And the quick

106

eared-rats pounced. They eat so many old books they
have to sick-up a few words every now and then:

TIME AFTER TIME, WORLD ENOUGH AND TIME, SLOW, SLOW, QUICK, QUICK,SLOW, AND DANCE TO E=MCSQUARE DANCE TIME

'Times's relative,' said the aged man again, 'On your
side of this fence it's moving but on the other side it's
stopped, I reckon. See, there's nothing but the bush,
outback, desert...'

I pondered on the nuance between *stopped* and *standing
still.* 'What is your name sir?' I asked.

'John, John Donne – spelled, D.O.N.N...'

'I know how it's spelled.' How did I know?

'Not Don John you understand, I'm not a philan-
derer.'

'I never thought... So time stops at this fence?' I
wanted to get back to the point.

'Right here, just rolls itself into a ball and all the
memories of the world are here under my feet. That's all
there is you know, a ball of tangled memories and the
world rushing blind towards this fence, then stopping
short, right on this line, running to a standstill.'

'I can't see a ball.'

'It's metaphysical.'

'I'd better ask my friend Leibniz,' I said. Leibniz was a
coypu and self-appointed leader of the rats.

Suddenly he was there. 'All that time-warping stuff is
nonsense, see they've all gone under the fence, there was
no stopping them, Hogarth, Hobbes, the billy goat, Leavis,
the ram, and all my rats.'

John Donne came down off the fence. 'They won't
come to any harm, people generally find their way back.

For them it might seem to take forever but to us it will be in no time at all. They will be back at precisely the same moment they went under which means they're already back somewhere around here. They won't have any recollection of actually having been anywhere.'

'You mean they've travelled into the future,' I said.

'If you like.'

'Impossible!' squealed Leibniz. 'That would mean travelling faster than light, impossible!'

'Clever rat you are,' said John, 'but wrong. You see the line, the fence, has length but no width at all; that's the definition of a line, so it takes no time at all to cross it.'

'But you said,' I joined in, 'we could never, ever, get past the fence, it sort of represents the present, it's a line between past and future.'

'It doesn't re-present the present Tim Bobbin. It *is* the present.' Then the chorus:

RE-PRESENT, REPRESENTATION, WE OFFER YOU OUR PRESENTATION, PRESENTLY WHICH IS TO SAY THE PRESENT IS NOTHING AT ALL BUT A REPRESENTATION OF ALL PASTS EVER PRESENTED UNTIL THE PRESENT, WORLD WITHOUT END, AMEN.

They were all back. 'Exactly correct,' smiled John.

ALL PRESENT AND CORRECT, sang the rats. I had to consult another expert; Berkeley, the rabbit, was an expert at disappearing tricks.

'I'm here,' squeaked the rabbit who was coloured silver and therefore invisible like a mirror. All one could see were rabbit-shaped reflections. Berkeley was also religious which was bound to confuse matters. 'I went over there with the others. You couldn't see any of us over there could you?'

'That would require time which doesn't exist over there,' chipped in John.

'Not quite right,' answered the rabbit. 'You couldn't see us because God wasn't looking over there. He hasn't created the future yet so you can't see it. The view you see of the other side is not what is there but merely what you expect to see, what you think should be there. Your brain and your eyes cannot see nothing. When we came back that's what we thought we had seen too; what we expected, what we imagined we had seen from this side. But we were really in a non-place, a nothingness. We can't remember because there is nothing to remember. Basic epistemology.'

'He means ontology,' snorted Leibniz. That set off the rats:

SCATOLOGY, SCATTERBRAINOLOGY, SATURDAY THEOLOGY, BLOGOLOGY, ONANOLGY, ON AND ON CODOLOGY

There was only one thing for it, I would find Blackamoor Coal and we'd go through the fence together. He was in bed with the alien, the Nomedian woman, Ellie. She was reading my thoughts, 'The rabbit's nearly got it but his god gets in the way. Unlike us Nomedians, you humans don't have the means to switch off your brains. You can't stop thinking and ninety percent of your thinking is useless. Mostly you take in data and you react to stimuli in a completely mechanical, uncreative way. You perceive, no you *receive* everything as facts when it's all just *ficts* – an infinite number of possible facts or none at all as in this case.'

I was baffled. 'Will you come with us Ellie, into the future?'

'I will see nothing,' she said, 'and you will see what you want to see.'

'We could try walking backwards,' said Leavis.

YING TONG IDDLE I PO, I'M WALKING BACKWARDS FOR CHRISTMAS, I'VE TRIED WALKING SIDEWAYS AND WALKING TO THE FRONT…

Presently they arrived at the fence. John Donne was unravelling his giant ball of string which he said was metaphysical. 'You see each strand is someone's life, a time line, but I can't find any loose ends.' Then up popped a kangaroo. 'This is Heidegger,' said John. 'Roos can't normally walk backwards.'

I scowled a warning to the rats. 'But he has a party trick.' On this cue the kangaroo leapt spectacularly over the fence and then straight back again and kept on doing it until he was exhausted. 'The point is,' said John, 'every time he crosses the line his time line snaps and I have a loose end and these are otherwise almost impossible to find.'

But then the roo winked and produced from his pouch a pair of scissors and cut the string. 'Now you have three loose ends,' he laughed and cut again and again and again. 'You thought you could follow it back into my history didn't you? Nonsense, see I can chop your ball to shreds, snip, snip, snip. You can no more go backwards than I can.'

'I didn't think male kangaroos had pouches,' said Hogarth the pig.

PIG IN A POKE, PIG IN A POKE

'We only have the present, we are the present,' said Heidegger the kangaroo. John was weeping and carefully collecting up the bits of string and placing them in a little tin box labelled, STANZAS.

All along the fence guards were appearing. Roman soldiers. 'The Italians,' choked Coal, 'The Mackeville Amateur Operatic Society.'

'Don't look like singers to me, they are oh so real,' said Ellie. 'Somebody doesn't want us getting in there. That kangaroo shouldn't have chopped up the string, he's let something out of the box, look, there's hundred, thousands, as far as you can see.'

'Chains, manacles, whips, the galleys,' muttered Coal, the escaped slave.

'Time for bed,' said Zebedee.

We turned and ran and ran, straight back down to the shitty little creek. It was going dark but we could just make out the dark outline of our whale.

Graham Chadwick

Theft

1 p.m.: Must remember the cornflakes. Wonder if Maud will call this afternoon. No doubt I'll get a blow by blow account of her trip to the chiropodist. Mr Williams doesn't seem his usual cheerful self. He barely acknowledged me when I came in. And that chap, he looks shifty. Don't like the look of him at all.

1.05 p.m.: Might as well get some milk whilst I'm here. Wonder if Mr Williams has noticed that chap. I'm sure he's up to something. Perhaps I should have a change from cornflakes. It's a long time since I had weetabix. No, I'll wait until it's on special offer.

1.10 p.m.: He's definitely dodgy. No basket and he keeps looking round to see if anybody's watching. Surely Mr Williams has seen him. Why doesn't he do something? Cornflakes it is then. I know. I've got that coupon. What was it for? Soup I think. Yes, I'll use it before it's out of date. Tomato or leek and potato?

1.15 p.m.: I was right. He's putting something into his pocket I'm certain. He hasn't paid and he's heading straight for the door. Cheek of it. It's people like him who put prices up. Stop him! He's a thief! Go on, challenge him. Don't just stand there.

* * *

1 p.m.: It's a slack day. Wonder why there's hardly anyone in today. Just Mrs Bradwell as usual. She's faffing about near the cereal shelves. Last of the big spenders she is.

Still, at least she hasn't deserted me for Tesco's and their free parking. Mind you, she hasn't got a car. If things get much worse I'll have to let Dawn go at the end of the month.

1.05 p.m.: Funny, I didn't notice that chap come in. He's gone down the far end out of sight. I'd better keep an eye on him. Mind you, I bet Mrs Bradwell's watching him. Yes, thought so. Watching him with her eagle eye.

1.10 p.m.: Can't see him now. I was right, Mrs Bradwell's on his case. She keeps looking at me. Obviously expects me to do something. What she doesn't realise is that I can't do anything until he's pocketed something. What's she waving about? Oh, I might have known. Another coupon.

1.15 p.m.: Oh my god! He's done it. Bold as brass. Obviously no intention of paying. Trouble is I can't nab him until he actually leaves the shop. I do wish Mrs Bradwell would leave it to me. He could turn nasty, have a knife. It's not worth it.

*   *   *

1 p.m.: Coast clear. Nobody about except some old dear. She doesn't count. Too busy clutching her Kelloggs and heading for the till any minute now. His lordship hasn't even noticed I'm here. Dozy git. Easy come, easy go, as they say.

1.05 p.m.: Come on love, shift it will you. Cereals – fridge – cereals. Just go for the Weetabix darling. Now he's got his beady eye on me. Thinks I'm going to cause trouble.

Too damned right I am. Not hanging about here for long. Gotta keep moving.

1.10 p.m.: Christ almighty! Why won't she leave me alone? Waving that piece of paper like a flag. Bog off. It's like centre court at Wimbledon. Looking from me to him and then back again. He can't back her anyway. Let's keep it that way man.

1.15 p.m.: Right! Half a bottle of Jamieson's snug in my pocket. Nice work. Nobody's noticed. Damn, Miss Bloody Marple's clocked me. Bet Mr 'Couldn't-care-less, I'm insured' won't risk it though. Move it woman, I'm off.

Barbara Oldham

Waiting In The Wings

Caroline pushes past Alison, sashays up the stone steps, flicking her scarlet umbrella open as she goes. Alison, still fuming from their earlier exchange, sticks out her tongue. She can already feel the rain seeping through her jumper, cooling her skin. The lane here at the rear of the theatre smells of musty drains and last night's chips, making her stomach lurch; water plops steadily from the stage door sign onto her dolly shoes, trickles between her toes. Caroline has disappeared now, headed towards the town centre. Alison shivers.

'Good riddance, snotty cow,' Alison announces to the empty street. She notices that the dreary overcast sky exactly matches the grey slate roofs as she glances back at the stage door. 'No point staying where I'm not wanted.' She trudges up the steps in Caroline's wake and stumbles at the top, landing heavily on one knee.

'Blast it.' Her new 15 deniers now have a ragged hole revealing a nasty graze. Alison takes deep breaths, waits for the stinging to subside. Then she limps down a side street rather than run the risk of bumping into Caroline. The narrow buildings here have brass plaques on their high frontages that glint at her like wolves' eyes as she passes. Her soles flap unevenly against the cobbles, echoing hollowly off the walls and she steps up her pace, knee throbbing, to get as far away as possible.

'Who the hell does she think she is anyway – Judy Dench?' she spits.

Alison goes over today's rehearsal, trying to make sense of Caroline's reaction to her (almost – when she thinks about it – brilliant) suggestion. She had been

thrilled when she'd been taken on for her first assistant
director's job – had totally immersed herself in the
production of Ibsen's 'Doll's House', reading it over and
over until the words and their meaning became part of
her. Watching Caroline transform into Nora during
countless rehearsals, Alison had visualised how the
claustrophobic atmosphere of Ibsen's play could be
cranked up to max. Only Nigel, the director, was always
so busy with 'Her Royal Highness' (as the backstage lot
called her) that she never got the chance to run her ideas
by him. Finally, at today's last rehearsal, she couldn't
suppress her thoughts any longer and had spoken up.
Caroline had glared at her, shouted for Nigel to 'get this
scruffy creature off my stage.' Then came the crocodile
tears. She'd wailed on about 'certain people' trying to
undermine her at the crucial stage of production; as
leading lady, of course she knew best. How, at the last
minute, was she supposed to rethink her stage choreogra-
phy? It would all but ruin her performance. To top it all
Caroline had then stormed out, firing off a parting shot:
never in her entire career had she been treated so
shabbily; they would all be sorry. 'I will not be treated like
an amateur in this tin-pot rep.'

Nigel watched Caroline go. 'Sorry Alison,' he said,
'I've got a lot riding on this, you'll have to make yourself
scarce.'

'But I was only trying to help.'

'Caroline's on a knife's edge – she won't listen to reason.' He shrugged. 'I'd better go after her.' Striding off
into the wings, he called out, 'Caro, Caro, please, wait a
moment…'

Alison sighed.

'You're right, you know.' Craig, the stagehand, stood

116

next to her, broom in hand.

'Why won't Nigel stand up to her, her and her pompous double-barrelled attitude?'

'Same old – stage politics. Nigel knows you're right but he's got to keep everybody happy. 'Specially her.' Craig put a reassuring hand on Alison's shoulder.

She shook it off. 'Sorry Craig, I think I need some air.'

'Don't do anything daft, Ali. You're the best assistant he's ever had.'

The rain is pelting down now. Alison kicks a can into the gutter and its saccharin contents splash up her legs. 'Damn and blast her,' she mutters, tears rising.

'Ooh, someone's got the 'ump.'

Alison spins round. A gangly teenager on a BMX bike, hood pulled up against the rain, grins at her then speeds off into the gloom.

'You should have lights on that thing,' she shouts after him. Darkness is closing in, she is soaked, and her knee still hurts. What is she doing here? Suddenly she feels the urge to get back to the theatre, pronto. But where is she? Going straight from digs to the theatre every day she hasn't found time to explore the town's maze of cobbled streets.

The wrought iron lamps above her head flicker into life. Grateful, she hurries to the end of the road. A garish neon sign glows like a beacon outside a newsagent's shop, a few doors down.

'What can I do you for, love?' the newsagent asks, peering through bottle thick glasses, as Alison flies through the door, almost knocking over a crisp stand.

'Sorry.' She points apologetically.

'No harm done,' he says, straightening the rack.

Alison spots the clock behind the counter. Just gone six.

'In a hurry, love? Most people seem to be these days.'

'I am actually. I've forgotten where I was. Or rather, where I came from.'

'Mm.' The man scratches his head.

'I'll take these.' Alison grabs a bottle of water and a packet of prawn cocktail crisps. 'I need to get to The Embassy Theatre. It's important.'

'I can see that.' His lenses twinkle. 'Stone's throw away, you are. End of the street, left, right, and Bob's your uncle. Or your human sat nav,' he chuckles, pointing at his name badge.

'Thanks Bob, you're a star.'

'Break a leg, young lady,' he calls after her as she hurries out of the shop.

The stage door is unlocked. Alison creeps up the stairs into the wings, stage left.

'Everyone back on stage,' Nigel commands, tapping on his clipboard, brow furrowed. 'Final words, ladies and gentlemen.' He nods in acknowledgement as his leading lady makes her entrance stage right, draped in a gold embroidered dressing gown. 'Caroline my dear, all well?'

'Where have you been?' Craig whispers in Alison's ear. 'Nigel's been doing his nut.'

'It's her that's nuts.' Alison glowers at Caroline, busy positioning herself in the spotlight.

'You're not wrong there. She only came back half an hour ago and she's already upset three people. Dawn's crying in the loo. Apparently madam's costume has mysteriously shrunk.'

Alison starts to shiver.

'Might have something to do with the two pasties and mushy peas she ate when she went out. And a Krispy Kreme. I found the bags stuffed in her bin.' Craig moves over. 'Here, get yourself dry, you're soaked.'

Alison leans against the old radiator. 'Thanks Craig,' she says, punching him lightly on the arm. 'You're a mate.'

They both laugh. Nigel glances in the direction of the disturbance, does a double take as he sees Alison and the corner of his mouth twitches.

'Suppose I'd better get my stuff,' Alison says, kicking at the time scuffed parquet, 'and dig out my CV.'

'Hang on Ali,' Craig urges.

'Nigel darling, about the furniture in Act One.'

Caroline's booming tone stops everyone in their tracks. They all watch, transfixed, as she begins to drag the prop furniture closer together, mindful of her recently manicured nails, until it teeters claustrophobically around the model doll's house, now dominating the stage – exactly as Alison had suggested.

'Voilà,' Caroline exclaims. 'This will make Nora's life appear more enclosed AND strengthen the doll's house metaphor.' Caroline weaves dramatically in and out of the furniture, practising her tarantella. 'A magnificent idea, don't you think?' she says, throwing her arms wide.

'Genius. Wish I'd thought of it.' Nigel winks at Alison.

Alison returns his wink, damp clothes and sore knee forgotten.

Nigel claps his hands. 'Curtain up in one hour. Let's go to it everyone.'

Claire Yates

119

Nineteen Fifty-Eight

A little talking,
Mostly quiet concentration,
Tunes carried home
Along safe pavements

Before she lost her way,
Changed her face,
Disappeared into the place
Where dreams are made.

Robert Smith

Clouds dark slate hang low
Leaden with moisture they droop
– Washing on the line

Claire Yates

Then and Now

Your soft skin smouldered
Once;
Radiance shimmered from passion
Once;
Your husky voice made me shudder
Once;
Well-deep, steadfast eyes gazed through my soul
Once

And I dared to caress, share your warmth,
Tilt my head to catch each jewel of nuance,
Memorise for eternity the message of that look

Now I suffocate, force myself to gasp
Breaths of silence not filling the void.
I drill commands at the telephone,
Wait and wait for your signature texts,
Check my e-mail inbox constantly. Each song
On the radio hums lyrics from your lips,
The old compact discs all bear your chosen imprint.
Outside, the sun tans where you nestled and
The breeze rustled your skirts, stirred your particular scent.
There is more. So very much more.

No more.

Martin Rimmington

The Remark

It costs him dear, that brief remark,
The light riposte that falls,
Leaden, at her feet.

Careless words strung like flags
Flap their way to the floor,
Puddling in a heap.

Eyes ice over, glassy lakes
Crazed by Arctic blast—
Jagged, frozen, deep.

Corneas flare cold, fix hard
In pointed, sharded glance
To kill his heat.

He watches, helpless, as she grinds her iceberg teeth.

Claire Yates

122

Promise: Katherine Mansfield's Final Adventure

Are you a reader? Do you read then…? Katherine's words seemed exiled from her mouth. These attempts at friendship were almost quaint these days and yet for the moment she wanted this coffee and this tablecloth with the bold tulip detail and yes, she wanted this woman to stay.

Two women with green baskets entered the cafe and sat over in the corner by the ancient dog.

The hands were busy at the sugar again and the old Katherine might have frowned at the distraction, but instead she smiled in her new faded way and held up her own spoon.

Try this – perhaps you might like… chestnut eyes for autumn and a sudden hand took her silver spoon and gently tapped her nose. One tap for yes, two for definitely, three for a whole day with me. Think carefully Ms Writer, you have just this minute to make up your mind.

Dark brown fire.

Katherine borrowed the spoon back and held the cupped end to her nose. She inhaled as gently as she dared. Warm metallic embers. Gardenia. The spoon moved once, twice and then, why not, once again. The magical promise of the three, the wisdom of the trinity. It was better than writing letters to those friends she would never meet again, better than watching the cat growing bored with her silent company. This was here, somehow a now had returned with the laces and the burnt chestnut eyes.

Wonderful! Your day can begin whenever you want it to. There will be no dawn or dusk until you decide. You are in perfect control of your, our destiny, Katherine.

If you say my name again I will cry.

But the woman didn't hear this thought and she said Katherine again and it didn't matter and it didn't matter that it didn't matter, because they had their day, all day.

Communion

There was a dark shape crouched on the ice. Katherine steadied her arm on her new friend and peered down at the small creature aware of her own need to sleep and the shape's utter stillness and silence. Was this death as it should be? Nothing moved around them: no urgent footsteps, no voices from the village. Just this outline of a life. Katherine closed her eyes and thought about praying and then knew that she could not.

When she opened her eyes again, the girl had knelt down, swaddling the animal in her scarf, her hair still touching the older woman's gloved hand. The creature faintly lifted a black face and took a look at them. One breath, one life. The girl lifted the creature into her coat and held on.

We need a box and straw and a fire. You have a fire too?

Mais oui.

All day long the help would build her sick mistress a small fire, promising better wood, less smoke. They were nearly there and the girl waited for Katherine to open the gate, and then the door, gestures that made the latter feel suddenly bold and brave. The fire was red and the girl settled the creature on the slate, calling to the maid for a saucer of water and honey. Now some chopped meat quickly.

Drink you. Eat this.

The girl started to loosen Katherine's boots and moved each toe slowly in the direction of the fire. Wisps of steam rose from brown stockings and for the first time in months, Katherine smiled.

Turnips.

They said there were the bones of the ancient dead feeding the vegetables here. Katherine turned her neck towards the wind stiffly thrilled by the rain.

One bite of a sweet turnip and you could be led somewhere, way back into the past, where faces were once slashed with blood red streaks, and voices sounded like this huge crow that stood watching her like a Victorian school master.

It seemed worth the risk.

Katherine shifted her boots and sniffed at the far away smell of stewed food, rehearsing a conversation she wanted to have with the stranger; perhaps she had forgotten how to speak to people. She hadn't even a name to call her yet and perhaps this was a good thing. Perhaps it was. For this was now a time for forgetting. (Her doctor had told her with his head on one side). For setting loose those names that anchored her to this muddy-grey mortal life. (Could she trust a man with plump pink hands?)

When she was younger, much younger, she had once practised talking into a mirror, changing her words, shaping her fringe and re-shaping her natural smile. There had been girls on the boat over who had assaulted everyone's ears with their fast chatter and Katherine had watched them like this crow, appalled. Yet her voice had always been slow, finding words and applying just the right amount of pressure to make them her own.

She bent down slowly and pulled up a small turnip, sweating with this new effort. They could eat it together.

Parting

There was nowhere to go. The woman stood watching tired leaves, thinking about her death. Nowadays it felt just one breath away. They had warned her, he had warned

125

her, everyone had spoken of the final haemorrhage; their safe clinical words separating themselves from this person she had now become. More leaves thrown up by the wind, a golden, bloodied carpet for a brief future and so many stories she would never write.

Never never never she whispered into a black woolly glove. Wet prayerless words. Now who had bought her such harsh luxury? She couldn't find the name, even when she shook her head listening at the past, and her mouth burned against the damp heat of the glove.

It was that coffee that had raised her up a little, had made her nod almost agreeably, but here she was alone again, shaking her head at the dissolving threads of memory. She pulled the hat lower over her cold ears. Muddy water skimmed over her boots, darkening them and a crow landed in front of her, its head on one side, calling to a companion she had not seen. If she was superstitious she would call this an omen, but this woman was less than any simple sadness today, yet more too.

For she had enjoyed the coffee, that synchrony of spoons and the face across the table, more than anything – she corrected herself – more than anything she had felt for a very long time. And it was time that she missed.

She missed the carelessness of health. She had written several stories she had enjoyed, yet her characters never seemed to do very much either. They lived small, tiny existences somehow. Always stood on steps or at windows looking in. But where could she have sent them that she would have believed in? There was nowhere.

Janet Lewison

Time Capsule

A memoir in five objects.

Shell: Gift of the sea, treasure from a childhood holiday, which reminds me of my parents, siblings and position in the family – my identity. With awareness of self there is also perception of other – everything else in the universe – which this shell represents. It is taken from my collection of found objects, each one of which denotes a particular walk, a unique time and place, and represents my special fascination with those things that are left behind, abandoned or discarded from nature.

External skeleton of some long dead sea-creature, it has been around for quite some time this small shell. Washed back and forth with every turn of the tides, faded, blurred at the edges and bearing the mark of encounters with others, which gives texture and rough hews it; we have some points of contact this shell and I.

Wedding Ring: Item of totemic power created of gold mined from the earth. The ring, symbol of eternity and the circle of life, also represents my status and position in society. Gold or golden has come to denote the most precious of things or the most favoured or blessed. The alchemists sought to transform base metals into gold, and so this makes it the metal associated with transformations or change. With this ring my life is changed forever to include others: we two, our children, our descendants.

Feather: Of air. I am not a birder, I am certainly not a twitcher. I watch birds and look for their shadow on the earth, I name them. This feather recalls a time when we were born not into a world of humans, but of animals. It connects me with my ancestors, who lived a life enriched by close proximity to the natural world and the intense observation of the animals on which their survival often depended; they identified with them, celebrated them in ritual, dance and rites of passage and revered them in myth and legend. Nowadays we do not live so close to nature and this can give us an intense longing to feel for ourselves that thrill of living alongside wild animals, to experience kinship with them. Some may satisfy this craving by keeping wild creatures as pets. For myself I am content with a walk in the countryside, all my senses alert and on the lookout for these, our shy contemporaries; then I know I am truly alive.

A piece of charcoal: Forged in fire, this is the medium I favour when I draw, and as such it represents my inner life. To draw from life involves the act of looking and forces you to engage in a meaningful way with another object or person; it involves time and memory, engages the senses and confirms what it is to be human. Drawing is a distinct and wholly human activity, chimpanzees and even elephants have occasionally demonstrated some ability to produce paintings, but can never be trained to draw.

Finally some theatre tickets: Souvenir of taking two children – my great-nephew and great-niece – to see 'Tom's Midnight Garden' at the Library Theatre for a Christmas treat. My husband, Tom, jokingly calls this 'buying immortality', I prefer to see myself as a memory maker, but it goes deeper, back in time to two other

128

children, sisters, and an unspoken pact. These childhood companions never knew either of their grandmothers, and that loss, in part, defined their early years. When a brother's children later suffered that same loss, one sister, the elder, stepped into the role. Now it is the younger one's turn with her grandchildren: it is my consolation.

The play did not disappoint. There is always something special about a live performance and this was a magical piece of theatre that, with minimal props and sets, was able to transport us to another time, another place. How much better to nurture a child's imagination than to spoon feed it with special effects that have the opposite effect.

So these are my five objects of contemplation, possessing qualities of the elemental, the alchemical and the magical. From them I derive what Virginia Woolf referred to as 'moments of being'; through them I gain knowledge of what I am or aspire to be – child, woman, animal, human and immortal.

Pam Hunter

Cancer

Briny, you scuttle in moonshine
to crab your past; touch and cling.
Rooted, your sensitive breasts still yearn
the silver of summer laughter,
dream of travel and adventure.
I long to open you, fulfil,
but you avoid, bury in your sandcastle,
so cautious, safe in the old.

Martin Rimmington

Memory

Gone
       From her room
Like glitter
       We stop
              To write it
       With red roses

Vicky Adshead

130

Listen

I just need a listening ear
Please, no clichés,
I won't hear.
Need a shoulder,
No advice.
Please, no judgements,
It's my life.

Are you listening?
Do you care?
Hold my pain
No need to stare.
I need time and empathy.
Please, be patient
With your sympathy.

There are times when we feel low.
The waves of grief
May ebb and flow.
Be there, stay there,
Listen well.
It's my story
I need to tell.

Chris Davenport

Time Out

Dear Miss Didcott,

I write in response to your advertisement in the Slitterthwaite and District Gazette, regarding your appeal for volunteers.

I am available one morning per week and would be pleased to assist with your 'Creative Ideas for Crafty Minds' sessions for adults in the Village Hall.

My particular areas of expertise are Quilling (exquisite little works of art formed using tiny rolled strips of paper) and Découpage (another paper delight, this using layered cutouts which are then lacquered), but I do have a keen interest in all things crafty and would be able to offer a wide variety of interesting and achievable ideas, projects and demonstrations.

I should be grateful if you would send me further details of your exciting project by post or e-mail. I look forward to hearing from you.

Yours sincerely,
Amanda Larming.
e-mail: ALarming-crafts@hotmail.com

*　　*　　*

Dear Miss Didcott,

Thank you for your e-mail. Wednesday mornings would be preferable to Monday mornings as I am currently attending an 'Introduction to Heritage Quilting' course run by Threadles of Chester on Mondays and Tuesdays, alternate weeks. Had you any particular times in mind? And for how many weeks would you be looking to run the

'Creative Ideas for Crafty Minds' sessions?

I'm not sure whether I am qualified to provide the certificate you are offering to the students – the original advertisement did not mention that this was to be a certificated course – but I am sure we can come to some arrangement.

I appreciate that you are unable to tell me exactly how many students to expect until you have received all the feedback from the organisations to which you sent the speculative survey, but a rough idea would be helpful regarding facilities, equipment and suitable activities. I look forward to hearing from you.

Yours sincerely,
Amanda Larming.

e-mail: ALarming-crafts@hotmail.com

P.S. I was a little taken aback by some of the organisations you contacted, but assume your questionnaire is aimed at their staff.

* * *

Dear Miss Didcott,

I was rather surprised to receive such a prompt reply to my e-mail, but I'm sure I will be able to organise the first session for next Wednesday, since you have already confirmed the date with the students. However, you make no mention of either materials (will you be providing these?) or scheduling (start and finish times, coffee breaks etc).

I should be grateful if you would contact me by return so that everything is ready and prepared for next week.

Yours sincerely,
Amanda Larming.

e-mail: ALarming-crafts@hotmail.com

Dear Miss Didcott,

Again, I am grateful for your swift response to my e-mail. However, I have to tell you that Macramé is not an area with which I am familiar, although I do agree with you that it is probably the easiest craft to provide at such short notice in terms of materials; the simplicity of one large ball of string and a couple of pairs of scissors is appealing. Sadly, I do not have the experience to transform these simple items into the decorative hanging basket holder with free-hanging tassels that you propose.

Please contact me at your earliest convenience with an alternative suggestion. Thank you.

Yours sincerely,
Amanda
e-mail: ALarming-crafts@hotmail.com

* * *

Dear Miss Didcott,

It seems we have our wires crossed. I did indeed mention my special areas of expertise, and one of them, as you quite rightly point out, was a foreign-looking word with accents. However, 'Découpage' is not the same as 'Macramé,' and therefore cannot be accomplished with a ball of string.

I have managed to put together a selection of simple materials ready for Wednesday and propose to demon-strate 'An Introduction to Greetings Cards.' This will give us a little time to order the more specialised materials that we will need for Découpage, and the students will then be able to use this technique in the production of the greetings cards. The whole thing will appear seamless! I am quite excited!

Yours sincerely,
Amanda

e-mail: ALarming-crafts@hotmail.com

*   *   *

Dear Miss Didcott,

I have just returned from the first meeting in the Village Hall with the Wednesday 'Creative Ideas for Crafty Minds' group.

I have to say that when I arrived at the venue, the number of police officers outside was rather off-putting, but it wasn't until I went into the Village Hall that I realised the purpose of their presence. Nowhere in the communications we have had to date is there any mention that the group would be entirely comprised of prison inmates, nor that they would be male. I suppose you have your reasons for withholding this detail from me, but at present, I am unable to even guess what those reasons might be.

I have now recovered sufficiently from the frisking I was subjected to by a particularly burly female officer at both the beginning and the end of the session. Whilst I had nothing to hide, it was imperative, she explained, that the six glue-sticks and dozen pairs of scissors with which I had arrived, should be accounted for before my departure. I didn't like to mention that we will need craft-knives at next week's session.

I would appreciate some support from you in this matter – would you be able to attend next week?

Yours sincerely,
Amanda

e-mail: ALarming-crafts@hotmail.com

Dear Miss Didcott,

Thank you for your e-mail and your explanation of the concepts behind 'Creative Ideas for Crafty Minds.'

Whilst I wholeheartedly support your good intentions in providing prisoners with opportunities for study and alternative life choices on their release, I'm not convinced that your proposed curriculum 'Découpage for the Desperate,' 'Quilling for Quick Fingers' or 'Macramé for Men' are particularly suited to this otherwise noble aim. As I mentioned in an earlier e-mail, I am not 'au fait' with Macramé, but in any case, the core material for this particular craft may prove a little too tempting to any of the students who might wish to make a bid for freedom, whilst taking a tightly bound hostage with them. As I appear to be the only suitable candidate in a potential hostage situation, I am unwilling to undertake the 'Macramé Made Easy' training course you suggest; let us not court danger. I hope you understand.

Yours,
Amanda

e-mail: ALarming-crafts@hotmail.com

P.S. You don't say whether you will be attending next week's session.

* * *

Dear Miss Didcott,

With regards to your recent e-mail; I feel your tone was a little hostile. I did not refuse to take part in any further training, nor was I totally insensitive to the needs of prisoners, as you suggest. Indeed, I seem to remember saying I supported your good intentions. However, there is a limit as to what can be achieved when the students in question are not serious candidates for the course upon which they have embarked. Jeering and slow hand-claps are not something I have experienced before in my craft sessions, and the language the men used inside some of the greetings cards was colourful, to say the least.

Since yesterday, I have had recourse to a considerable portion of my stock of Chateau Cantermerle 1999, which I was saving for my birthday party next month. I will not confess to how much of this was required to restore my shattered nerves; suffice it to say that I shall be obliged to place a substantial order at the end of this week to replenish my store.

As you have declined to attend next week's 'Creative Ideas for Crafty Minds' session, I feel under no obligation to be there either.

Yours,
Amanda
e-mail: ALarming-crafts@hotmail.com

Anne Lawson

Reflections

The girl sits in front of the mirror, hands resting on scabbed knees peeping from beneath the hem of her dress. Chosen by her mother, it has a pattern of tiny mauve and pink flowers, a scooped collar stiff with white lace. The bow digs into her back against the chair and she can feel the bite of gathered elastic around the puffed sleeves. Her forearms are bare apart from a sprinkling of summer freckles, matched by those that spill across her nose on to rounded cheeks. A plain gold clip restrains the ginger curls framing her clear blue eyes, the colour of forget-me-nots, that stare into the mirror.

She is planning to run away from home. There is no particular reason; it is rather that, having devoured numerous Willard Price stories borrowed from the library, she is keen to have an adventure of her own. She is taking the big bike she got last Christmas; it is cobalt blue, has its own stand and a sturdy wicker basket that buckles on to the handlebars with two leather straps. Next to the right brake is a large silver Mickey Mouse bell with a loud enough 'ding' to make her friends jump when she pedals at high speed out into the cul-de-sac. The strips of empty cereal boxes she cut up and pinned to the spokes with clothes pegs (the faster you go the more it roars like a motorbike) will have to come off.

She will leave when her parents are in bed; put on a t-shirt, the tank top her mum knitted, jeans, and, finally, her school plimsolls, as they won't squeak on the lino. The shed key is kept in the wooden pot next to the fish tank in the hall; it is full of old pennies, ring nuts and fuses, coiled up pieces of string. Dodgem, the goldfish she won at the fair, will see her take the key – but she knows he would never tell.

Opening her satchel, she takes out her furry pencil case and the exercise books covered in old wrapping paper; she won't need these again until September. She stuffs her Bazooka Joe torch into the front pocket; paid for in saved up tokens, it has an angled head and the option of a flashing red light. Alongside this she slips in the penknife bought with pocket money in Newquay whilst on holiday. In the main compartment she puts: an apple picked from the garden; a packet of garibaldi biscuits found at the back of the larder; and a carton of Kia-Ora saved from a trip to the Odeon with Nana to see The Aristocats.

She will go tonight. The only part of the plan she hasn't quite worked out yet is how she will carry Cuddles, her Toffo-coloured pet rabbit.

Claire Yates

A Web

After we lost the baby
She asked me to catch
a spider on a piece of paper
(so it would be untouched)
and she stood beside me
with an old tobacco tin
ready to press the lid
hard shut before it could
crawl out back to a womb
of dark safety.

We took the tin up to
the stark granite outcrop,
high on the desolate moors.
I trudged ahead across
the purple heather
with a rusty spade
trying to look
inconspicuous. If
anyone had asked
I was digging for gold;
'*Bright prospects*', I'd say.

The fiery low sun
illuminated our way
but cast eerie shadows
that menaced behind us.
The sun glinted on the
tin gripped in her hand.
I wondered if the

spider was dead. I
didn't want to be held
Responsible.
It was a natural event
I told myself repeatedly
as I dug deep into
the soft, cold, black
peat, and she muttered
incantations, fingered the
looming rock with signs.
She placed the tin in the dank
grave, and we both scattered
peat on to the lid,
invisible in the gloaming.
We made a tiny crucifix
from twigs and slivers
of wood, then stayed,
silent, until a new moon
rose, and its faint light
lit upon the shiny handle
of the redundant spade
where a bulbous spider
was weaving a web,
and a silky dew-laden thread
twitched imperceptibly
across to the granite.

No-one else had seen
or knew.

No-one was deceived.

Martin Rimmington

Unity

body hanging leaf-like
   on old tree dead
      far on the line of horizon swaying
gently turning
   a breeze sheds memories
      with skin

the tree, in death is strong
   the body hangs frail breaking
      identity is lost to both
as tree and flesh
   caress their
      returning.

Vicky Adshead

Dew glistens on grass
Cows steam, trampling as they munch
Curlews wheel aloft

Claire Yates

Walking the Past

Hello. My name is Evie. What's yours?

I'm twelve. I live in a cottage down the hill at the bottom of the moor with my dad. If you look back down there, past the bushes and to the left of that tree, you can just see the chimney and a bit of the roof. There, see?

It's a lovely day, isn't it? You look tired. Have you walked all the way up here? It's steeper than it looks. It fair wears most walkers out. Not me though, I'm used to it. I'm up here every day in summer checking the sheep higher up the hillside. When I was little my dad would bring me, but once I turned ten I could look after myself and I always come on my own now. It feels like I've looked after the sheep forever. I know them all by name, all forty-seven of them. Of course, dad doesn't know I've given them all names, he'd think I'm daft. It's my little secret. You won't tell?

Here, sit down for a bit and catch your breath. Where are you going? Is that a map you've got? That's pretty. I've not seen one like that before. I don't need a map; know these moors like the back of my hand.

Where did you say you were headed? Ah, the house. Well, of course, it isn't there now. And it wasn't a house to start with, you know. *They* called it 'Roynton Cottage,' after the village, but folks round here just called it 'The Bungalow.' I suppose when they added the second floor, it wasn't a bungalow any more, but the name stuck. It was a grand place, all made of wood, with great big windows looking out on every side.

You can see for miles on a clear day from up here, you know. You ever been to Blackpool? Well you can see

143

Blackpool Tower from up here when there's no smog. Twenty-five miles away it is. My dad told me. Fair walk that'd be. I reckon the grand people at the Bungalow sat in their parlour and looked out at the Tower on a clear day.

Have you got a parlour? Bet you can't see Blackpool Tower from yours, can you?

Sorry, was that insolent? My dad hates it. He'd leather me if he knew.

Are you ready to walk on? Shall I show you where the Bungalow was? It's not far; come. I'll take you. Do you know its story? It was always full of people in the summer, especially at weekends. Toffs with cars up from the big cities. They'd go shooting on the moors in the day and have parties at night.

How do I know? I could see them when I was minding the sheep from further up the hill. My dad said I wasn't allowed to go anywhere near the Bungalow or there'd be Big Trouble, but I'd get as close as I could without being seen and I'd sit and watch.

Beautiful dresses the ladies had, all the colours of the rainbow. And at night, the men were all dressed up like penguins. Very smart, but I couldn't help giggling at the sight.

One night, a night in July it was, I saw the people come out all dressed up and drive away, so when it grew dark enough, I sneaked into the grounds. You must never tell my dad; it'll be our secret. It was deathly quiet; no-one about. I just wanted a closer look. The sheep could do on their own. I crept right up to the Bungalow. It was scary, because I didn't want to get into Big Trouble, but it was exciting too. You ever felt like that? Your heart is fighting to get out of your body and you can't breathe, but your

144

mind feels oddly clear and carefree and filled with wild delight. It's a strange feeling, isn't it?

I tiptoed up to a window and peeped inside. It was fabulous – huge rooms full of carpet and curtains and furniture and beautiful pictures on the walls. Our cottage would fit into one room! I moved quietly all the way round peering into every room. It was lovely. There were ornaments on carved tables, flowers in great big vases and fireplaces you could roast a pig in.

But then I heard footsteps. I had to find a hiding place and quick! I spotted a trapdoor covering the coal-chute by the wall. I opened it and scrambled down.

It was really dark in there. I was frightened, I can tell you, but more frightened of being caught and getting into Big Trouble. So I stayed quiet. I held my breath when the footsteps tapped over the chute cover, but no-one guessed I was just below. Two people were whispering quite loudly, a man and a woman arguing. She won, though. She told him to leave straight away, so she could get on with it – she didn't want him to get the blame – and I heard his footsteps running off down the driveway.

I waited. It felt like forever. I wished she'd go.

I suppose I must have nodded off in the end, because suddenly, I couldn't think where I was. There was a strong smell of paraffin and stale smoke. It wasn't dark in my coal-hole any more. The cover had gone and above my head, fluffy white clouds danced across a pale blue summer sky.

Put me in mind of my sheep and I leapt up in a blind panic. What would my dad say if they'd wandered?

It was a struggle to get out of the coal-hole – I was stiff and cold and my body didn't seem to belong to me anymore. When I did finally heave myself out, the

Bungalow was gone, burnt to the ground.

Haven't been home since. Watched my dad grieve for me, though. He's dead now. Died of a broken heart in 1916, three years after the fire. You won't tell, will you?

Footnote In 1913 Lord Leverhulme's bungalow at Rivington Pike was burned to the ground by Edith Rigby, an English suffragette. The Bungalow was empty at the time.

Anne Lawson

Mother

After you're gone the bevelled mirror
Still reflects your presence;
I stare intently into its glaze
Catch your shadow over my shoulder.

I spin round, face your time-worn chair,
Softly chatter inanities, inform you of events,
Pretend you're feigning boredom, playing games,
Asleep… No, *not* asleep.

I wheel back, vision blurred, lick away
The trickles, sense my last kiss
To your wrinkled forehead, and peer at myself
Until I find refuge, comfort in your likeness.

Martin Rimmington

How Long We Lie

And don't forget how long we lie
In graves un-beautied hand
Our eyes downcast and blind are closed about the land
Far from the ears of love's sweet song
The body falls and breaks
To be swept and tossed upon the days
By wind's unthinking hand

Vicky Adshead

Time

Time is a dominant value in modern Western society. It is assumed to be clock time, an absolute linear measure where each hour has sixty minutes. We can either use this time, or lose it ('waste' it), and we can attribute a monetary value to it, as in 'The pay is £15 per hour.'

We use time as a tool to organise our lives, rising – say – at 7 am, working until 6 pm, and going to sleep at 11 pm. The fact that these periods correspond with light and dark is no mere coincidence; when the sun was our main light source it was sensible to follow its pattern.

However there are people for whom time is organic, dictated by the seasons. Farmers wake with the sun, so their rising is at slightly different times throughout the year. Fishermen must work when the tides are right and the weather is suitable. Because time in these cases is tied in with the flow of events, rather than merely the time on the clock, time becomes a matter of synchronicity rather than the fact that a measured period of time has passed. For these people, therefore, work begins when conditions are right, and stops when it is impossible to carry on. This is closer to the Hebrew sense of 'appointed' time or 'opportunity'. Time becomes cyclic, rather than a linear measurement.

Time is sometimes considered to be the Fourth Dimension, as without Time our lives would be static. It is our way of keeping track of the changes which are constantly happening in our universe. It could be said that Time only arises because of the dynamic nature of the universe, or perhaps it is the other way around, and the dynamism of the universe is only possible because there is Time!

Time means that things do not all happen at the same moment – in the same way that space prevents things all happening in the same place.

So – by Time we mean a series of changes or events which occur. Some of these events happen periodically, such as the sun rising and setting and the earth revolving around the sun, but our clocks – both real and biological – are synchronised with these cyclical events in order to keep track of what we call Time.

Audrey Rostron

Author Biographies

Anne Lawson
Anne finds it ironic writing about time, as it's the one thing she's always short of: too many interests that she is always threatening to pare down. But doesn't.

Audrey Rostron
Audrey was 75 in May 2011. She has lived through one world war, fifteen Prime Ministers, had two husbands, two sons and three careers, and has two stepchildren and five grandsons. She knows that in the mirror she will see Time has passed, but inside is still the same person.

Barbara Oldham
Barbara is growing old disgracefully whilst wearing purple. She enjoys theatre-going, languages and visiting new places. Under pressure she confesses to being something of a stationery-aholic with a vast pencil collection.

Chris Davenport
Chris is a perpetual teenager (well, in her head anyway). An 'outdoorsy' person who enjoys walking, ornithology and sport, her other interests include writing children's stories, watercolour painting and holding back time with anti-wrinkle creams.

Claire Yates
A serial gazer out of windows where nothing is impossible, she likes neologisms and good grammar. Claire finds her writing inspiration whilst out running with her dog. However, this always carries the risk that the breeze may catch her best ideas before she can get pen to paper.

Graham Chadwick

Graham has been writing for 60 years in all forms and genres. He says that his best work has always happened when he's been in a writers' group and he's been in plenty – from the Lancaster University M.A. programme to the French Nomedia Sci-Fi project. This Horwich group is brill.

Janet Lewison

Janet is an ex-university lecturer, who lives in Horwich with her family and lurcher dogs. She loves Katherine Mansfield, Sherlock Holmes and Dickens. She also runs Tusitala Tuition and writes a blog for Carol Ann Duffy's new Sheer Poetry site.

Martin Rimmington

An allusive, elusive, elliptical enigma who cherishes words – their sounds, order, meanings and sense – whether on paper, or song, or even semiologically, and who deplores all forms of injustice that so often deny the free word (not withstanding that a smile or a hug can render words superfluous).

Pam Hunter

A founder member of Phoenix Writers, Pam lives in Bolton and has a studio in Rossendale, where she practises painting, ceramics and printmaking. Her work references the natural world and this informs her writing. Pam is also a keen bridge player and sudukoholic.

Robert Smith

Robert started off studying chemistry, but preferred the alchemy of classical music, playing the piano and the great outdoors. His love of literature inspired him to join the writing group in order to create his own. A gentle thoughtful man, whose positive outlook radiated to those around him.

Vicky Adshead

The fleetingness of things (impermanence), our illusion of ownership, is often my inspiration. I find it in human emotion, the cycle of a flower – any experience in a day. So much has changed while you read these words...